THE WILL TO WIN
and Other Stories

STOPPED THE BALL'S BULLET-LIKE RISE WITH HIS
HUGE HANDS

The Will to Win
and Other Stories

BY STEPHEN W. MEADER

ILLUSTRATED BY JOHN GINCANO

SOUTHERN SKIES

SOUTHERN SKIES

LITTLE ROCK, ARKANSAS
www.southernskies.com

Dedication

The republication of this book is dedicated with love to Richard Kenneth Fellows--- athlete, sports authority, confidante, and loyal and loving friend of 45 years---by his best friend, Jerry Atchley.

TABLE OF CONTENTS

LIST OF ILLUSTRATIONS

THE WILL TO WIN

and Other Stories

COW-PASTURE BACKFIELD

THE GLOOM in the locker room of Cedar Creek High School that June afternoon was so thick you could cut it with a knife. The dozen boys gathered there had stopped clearing out their athletic equipment and were standing around in attitudes of dejection.

"Gosh!" groaned Skeets Haley, throwing an old baseball shoe on the floor with a clatter. "Why couldn't they wait one more year, till I graduate?"

"And that schedule we've got for next fall!" Peewee Gates put in. "What are we goin' to do—cancel all our games?"

"I know, it's too bad," Jim Lowden answered, "but they just haven't got the money. I asked Dad if they couldn't find some other way, but I guess it's no use."

It was Jim who had brought the bad news. His father was on the School Board, and at their meeting the night before, the Board had decided that an athletic coach was a luxury Cedar Creek couldn't afford. That meant that Jack Wickham, former State University halfback, would lose his job, and all their hopes for a winning football team would go a-glimmering.

The door opened, closed again, and an erect, square-jawed young man stood there smiling at them.

"Put away the crying-towels," he said. "No use feeling bad about it. You can't blame the taxpayers."

There was a heavy silence, broken at last by Russ Green, football captain-elect. "Gee, Coach," he blurted, "you know how hard this is to take. You're a sport, all right, but we wanted to show you some real football this fall. Now it's all off."

"Why?" Wickham snapped the word out like a challenge. "You've got eleven football players," he went on. "You've learned the fundamentals. If you're willing to do what I tell you, you won't have any cause to hang your heads."

The boys stared at him, uncomprehending. "You mean—we could go ahead without coaching—work up our own plays an' everything?" asked Peewee.

"You wouldn't have to," Wickham replied. He sat down on a bench. "Look here," he said, "I heard about this thing last night, and did some thinking before I went to sleep. This morning I got a job for the summer, so I'm all right. They'll take me on as sports director at the C.C.C. camp, over on Big Baldy. You live up that way, don't you, Haley?"

"Sure," Skeets nodded. "Our back pasture runs right

up to the foot of the mountain. Russ Green's near there, too—an' Chick Harrison."

"Our farm's only a mile this side," put in Beany Singer, the rangy end.

"Good!" said the ex-coach. "How many of the rest of you could get there—say a couple of afternoons a week, this summer?"

All but one or two were local farm-boys. Except in haying-time, they thought they could make it.

"Let's see, now," Wickham pursued, jotting names on a piece of paper. "We'll have a backfield, anyhow. Peewee Gates, quarter—Lowden and Skeets Haley, halves—Russ Green, fullback. For ends we've got Beany Singer and Chick Harrison. Walt Evans and Bob Lewis, left tackle and guard—you can get there? And how about you, Goat? We're going to need a center."

Goat Walker scratched his red head. "I'll be workin' in the store, same as usual," he said. "Still, I reckon I could get the delivery truck for two afternoons a week. That way I could pick up these two big lummoxes here—" he indicated Arne and Ole Nelson.

The Swedish brothers grinned their wide, slow grins. "We bane come even if we walk," said Arne.

"Hooray for the plow-oxen!" shouted Peewee, slapping their broad twin backs. "That takes care o' the right side o' the line, an' we're all set."

"Haying ought to be out of the way by this time next month," Wickham said. "That'll give us six weeks of practice before school starts again. I probably shan't be around here after that, and I won't be able to get to all your work-outs, but I'll give you everything I can while I'm there."

He paused, looking around at them. "This season of yours means a lot to me," he said. "I started you slow last fall, just to let you get the feel of a football. We only had three games and lost two of them, but that was all right. I was building for this year. And I don't propose to have those plans knocked in the head by a little thing like being fired. So we'll meet in Skeets Haley's cow-pasture the last Wednesday in July. That suit everybody?"

There was an earnest chorus of assent. The gloom had lifted, when, by ones and twos, the boys drifted off, shouting their good-bys.

Russ Green and Skeets Haley were the last to leave. "Feelin' better?" asked the husky fullback.

"Say—maybe I'm not!" Skeets responded. "All I ask is another crack at that Paxton bunch, with their flossy silk pants an' All-American coach. After last fall's 45-0 walloping I heard one of 'em say a little school like Cedar Creek had no business on their schedule!"

"Yep," said Russ, "it would be fun to crack their line for a touchdown. But we've got a lot of work to do before that happens."

.   .   .   .

Mid-August was clear and cool, in that northern valley. Wheat and oats were ripening to gold in the sun, and the blackberry vines by the roadside were bending with glistening fruit, as Chauncey Dale drove his roadster up the trail to Big Baldy. He lolled back behind the wheel and joined his agreeable tenor with Joe Stein's bass.

"Isn't Cedar Creek up here somewhere?" asked Stein, when the song was ended.

"Sure," laughed Dale. "That last cross-roads we passed. There were a couple o' trees in front o' the town. That's why you didn't see it." He continued to chuckle as he guided the car into a narrow wood-road. "Remember that game? Why, some of 'em didn't even have cleats on their shoes!"

Joe Stein, whose father owned Paxton's biggest department store, grinned reminiscently. "I hear they've lost their coach," he said. "If they're saps enough to play us again this year, we ought to run up a hundred points!"

Chauncey Dale yawned. "Why make so much effort for so little glory?" he asked lazily. "We'll save the steam roller for some of the games that count. Say, you might be getting out those fishing-rods. The lake isn't far, now."

The car was moving slowly along the rutted track. On one side were woods, and on the other, beyond a fence of rusty barbed wire, was an old pasture dotted with blueberry thickets, birch saplings and jack-pine. Suddenly Dale put on the brakes and slid to a stop.

"What was that?" he exclaimed. "Did you hear somebody yell?"

They switched off the motor and sat there listening. From somewhere in the pasture, close at hand, they heard a high voice barking—"Eight—twenty-three—nineteen—hip!" There was a momentary silence, then more cries. "Take him out! Here it comes, Chick!"

And before their astonished eyes a brown oval shot out from behind a birch clump and sailed in a clean arc over the tall juniper bushes. An agile figure in overalls leaped high in the air and snared the flying missile. They caught half-glimpses, through the brush, of quickly moving figures. And after a few seconds there was another yell. "Good tackle, Goat! Got him low. Made forty yards on that one!"

Chauncey Dale turned and looked into his companion's mirthful face. "Well, I'll be—" he murmured, and slapped his thigh. "Come on, Joe, this is too good to miss."

There was plenty of cover in the pasture to conceal their stealthy advance. They crept through a jack-pine thicket and found themselves at the edge of an irregular open space where a dozen boys in nondescript farming clothes were gathered. Some of the younger ones were bare-footed. Others had on sneakers. Two of the tallest—big, hulking blonds—wore cowhide boots.

"Say," whispered Stein. "I've seen that red-haired one before. Didn't he play center on—"

"Sure," Dale replied, half choked with laughter, "—don't you know what this is? It's the Cedar Creek football team. Oh, boy—oh, boy! Look, they're lining up!"

Goat Walker was crouched over the ball, flanked, on one side only, by the Nelsons and Beany Singer. Opposite them the left side of the line was arrayed for defense. Gates, Haley, Lowden and Green were in single wing-back formation, and three or four smaller urchins composed what must have been meant for a defensive backfield.

Peewee Gates was calling signals again, and the ball came back. The instant he had snapped it, Walker helped Arne Nelson block out the opposing left guard. Then, to the watchers' amazement, he swung around and charged into the backfield, obviously bent on smearing the play. He was stopped by the small but wiry form of the quarterback. With Green and Lowden ahead of him, Skeets Haley carried the ball on a slice off tackle. Chick Harrison, defensive end, had been boxed out, and the small fry were quickly bowled over by the interference. Skeets side-stepped a juniper bush, straight-armed a jack-pine, and fooled a moss-covered stump with his change of pace. He was goal-line bound —if there had been a goal-line.

The two young men from Paxton might have witnessed another hour of this astounding spectacle if they had not been overcome with merriment. As it was, Dale was so carried away by Haley's touchdown run that he prevailed on his companion to lead a cheer. The deadly seriousness of the little squad's practice was interrupted by a hysterical chant from the near-by thicket. "Wah-hoo! Wah-hoo! Wah-hoo! Rackety-rax! Cedar Creek!"

Russ Green strode over with a face like a thundercloud. The pair who crawled out of the brush were convulsed with laughter, tears running down their cheeks, but he recognized them at once as members of the lordly Paxton outfit.

"Think it's funny?" he growled in a cold fury.

Chauncey Dale shook his head weakly. "No," he said.

"It's colossal! Thanks for the entertainment. Come on, Joe."

And they walked back to their car, leaving an angry and uncertain crew of farmer-boys standing in the pasture.

"Just for that," said Goat Walker, through gritted teeth, "I hope we play 'em on a wet field. Would I like to rub that stuck-up bird's face in the mud!"

The roadster rolled off up the road, and they saw no more of their visitors. But two days later the sports columnist of the Paxton *Star* outdid himself in humor. He had recognized the news value of the yarn brought in to him by two prominent members of the high school social set, and he made the most of it. Under the head-line "Cow-pasture Backfield," he gave his readers a facetious description of the Cedar Creek team in train-ing—not forgetting the line's doubling act, or the role played by the trees, stumps and bushes.

The story was picked up by other papers, and for a week the lives of the makeshift squad were miserable indeed. One enterprising news photographer even made a trip to the foot of Big Baldy, but all he got was a land-scape picture. The boys were not there. Knowing their predicament, Jack Wickham had obtained permission for them to practice on the C.C.C. camp field.

"Listen," he told them grimly. "Your chance to

laugh may come yet. You've really learned something this summer. Throwing and catching passes in a cowpasture may be funny but it isn't easy, and I like the way you're handling that ball. Now let's get down to those plays. I'm only giving you about half a dozen, but that's enough. You've got a slow line but one that'll hold. That means your passers won't be rushed—and it's in the air you've got to win if at all."

In early September they had one practice game with the C.C.C. boys before their season opened. It was the last time Wickham could be with them. He had been engaged as coach by a high school farther down the state.

There was no regular scoring allowed in the game, but when it was over their mentor looked pleased. Outweighed by the huskies who opposed them, the Cedar Creek lads had more than held their own. Twice Jim Lowden and Skeets Haley had been put in the clear for what would have been certain touchdowns. Their interference formed smartly. Their passes were fast and reached their mark. Some of Russ Green's punts traveled fifty yards.

Before they left for home, Jack Wickham shook hands all round. "I'll be pulling for you," he said soberly. "You're my team, even if I'm not your coach. You'll have to play sixty minutes of every game with no replacements to speak of. Iron man stuff. But I think you've got what it takes. Good-by, all."

.   .   .   .

The Paxton game was scheduled for the third week in October. Cedar Creek had opened with Jonesville, and won by a 6-0 score. However, as Jonesville was notoriously weak, the victory occasioned little comment. Greenfield—the second game—was different. They met a big, experienced team, played them off their feet in the first half, then hung on grimly to emerge with the long end of a 12-7 count.

"Cedar Creek?" people asked themselves. "Isn't that the team that practiced in a cow-pasture? Say—maybe they're not such rubes, after all!"

And so, that Saturday of the Paxton game, there were a lot of cars on the road. From up and down the county, people were heading for town. Jolting along on planks laid across Jim Lowden's farm truck, the Cedar Creek squad waved laughingly to familiar faces in the passing autos.

"Well, anyhow," crowed Peewee Gates, "they won't have to be ashamed of our uniforms." Carefully washed and darned, there were fourteen jerseys and twelve pairs of football pants in the bottom of the truck. By saving and scrimping, they had also rounded up enough cleated shoes to outfit the team.

They reached Paxton before noon. There the gang repaired to a lunch-wagon near the railroad tracks and made such a meal as they could off hamburgers and fried egg sandwiches. "Ugh!" Chick Harrison growled as he came out. "Greasy grub! I feel as if I'd swallowed a cannon-ball!"

"Just nervousness," Haley reassured him. "You'll get over it when the game starts."

Goat Walker, who could eat anything, laughed at them and munched the remains of his third sinker. "That's what I call a meal," he announced. "Bring on your Paxton sissies! I'm ready for 'em now."

They found a place to park the truck near the high school field-house, and were led to their dressing-room by a supercilious assistant football manager. "You can use these lockers," he said. "Showers are over there. It's Saturday, so some of you might want to take a bath after the game." And he departed before they could think of any adequate reply to this bit of sarcasm.

There wasn't much to do, there in the dark little dressing-room. Slowly they disrobed and got into their football togs. There was no laughter and little talk. Occasionally one would look at his watch and scowl. "Quarter o' one. 'Most an hour before we can go out." Then a relapse into fidgety silence.

Finally they heard a quick step in the corridor outside. The door swung open and Jack Wickham stood there smiling.

"Hm!" he said. "What is it—a wake? Somebody break a leg? Snap out of it, gang!"

They were all on their feet. "Gosh, Coach! How'd you get here?" gasped Russ Green. "We're sure glad to see you!"

"Just sitting here worrying, eh?" Wickham grinned. "Guess it's a good thing I came! My team played yesterday and we're meeting Paxton in two weeks. So I'm here to scout 'em. Maybe you won't mind if I sit on your bench? Say, how's that 'thirty-three' play going?"

The blues had vanished as if by magic. Eagerly they discussed plays—weaknesses that had developed in their first two games—and how they planned to overcome them. Wickham listened and advised. Twenty minutes before game time he stood up briskly.

"Don't be surprised if they razz you a bit out there," he said. "Just close your ears and concentrate on football. You can take it. All right—let's go!"

Trotting the hundred yards from the dressing-room to the field, the Cedar Creek squad became aware of several things. First was the crowd—far larger and noisier than any they had played before. Hoots and cat-calls and roars of laughter heralded their entrance. There was a big cloth sign tacked up on the fence under the score-board, with the words "COW-PASTURE BACKFIELD" in letters two feet high. And as the eleven first-stringers lined up to run through signals, a raucous *tonk-a-tonk* from hundreds of cow-bells broke out in the Paxton stand.

Halfway down the field, Jim Lowden fumbled a pass from center. The jeers redoubled. "Give it to me again!" snarled Jim under his breath, and the team snapped into position. The ball came back and he handled it flawlessly on a spinner through tackle. The squad's taut nerves relaxed. They were grinning and kidding each other by the time they reached the goal-line. There they broke up to toss passes and catch punts while the big red-shirted Paxton crew took the field.

As game time neared they went back to their bench, empty except for Wickham and the three lonely substitutes. "Receive, if you win the toss," the ex-coach told Russ Green. "Cut loose right from the whistle and you'll catch 'em off balance."

The captain nodded and went out to meet the referee. The big, black-haired fellow in the red jersey who stood beside him gave Russ a lazy smile. "Believe we've met before," he said. "I'm Joe Stein."

The Cedar Creek boy shook hands. "Yes," he answered. "I remember." He called heads and the coin fell tails. Stein grinned again exasperatingly. "No wind, to speak of," he said. "We'll kick off to you."

"Thanks," replied Russ. He chose the south goal and the two teams took their positions. In the Cedar Creek scheme of defense it was the slippery Skeets Haley who acted as safety man. He was lucky on that first kick-off. It came down low and fast, bounding right into his hands on the twenty-five-yard line. There was little time for interference to form, but Green took out the first tackler and Skeets side-stepped another to reach the thirty-five before he was downed.

Without a huddle, the country boys jumped into their places. Peewee Gates barked out a quick series of numbers. With the snap of the ball Lewis and Evans, on the left side of the line, charged low and opened a three-foot hole. And Russ Green went crashing through on a straight line-buck for nearly ten yards. Second down and one to go on the forty-four-yard line. It was obvious to everybody that they'd run another line play to make that yard. The Paxton secondary, caught flat-footed on the first play, came up hastily. And Peewee was calling signals again.

This time the ball went to Lowden. He dropped back two paces, coolly watching Skeets Haley and the ends as they sped up-field. His pass, unhurried, traveled thirty yards in a clean spiral and Beany Singer projected his long arms aloft to take it. There was a Paxton back close, but not close enough. Beany made the catch. A second later, just as he was about to be tackled, he tossed the ball back to Haley, on his flank, and Skeets was off like a flash. Only the safety man remained in front of him, and Chick Harrison was running interference.

The Paxton quarterback looked big and capable. Chick didn't have the weight for a blocker, but he sailed in nevertheless. And then he caught sight of the confident leer on the defense man's face. It was Chauncey Dale. The fiery little Cedar Creek end clenched his teeth and catapulted his body across Dale's legs. He was dizzy when he picked himself up, but he could see Skeets Haley's green jersey across the goal-line.

A touchdown in two plays! There was consternation in the Paxton stands, and cheering from the up-county farmer-folk. The Cedar Creek boys gathered in a huddle. They knew their own weaknesses and one of them was goal-kicking. There hadn't been much chance to practice that art in the pasture below Big Baldy.

"Make it a flat pass over the line," urged Peewee Gates. "You go back for the kick, Russ, an' Jim'll act like he was goin' to hold it. I can sneak through there if Goat'll make a hole for me."

They took their places and Walker snapped the ball

back to the half-kneeling Lowden. Then his stocky legs shot him forward like steel springs. He caught the opposing center amidships with a billy-goat butt, and Peewee slipped through behind him. In the same second the ball spun over the line like a bullet from Jim's lifted arm. The little quarterback clutched it close and went down under a landslide of tacklers. Cedar Creek had seven points.

Naturally, the surprise strategy couldn't be expected to work twice. The farm-boys received again, but this time, after two ineffectual stabs at the line, Russ Green sent off a high, sailing punt to the enemy's forty-yard stripe. Then the battering began. The Paxton players were big and heavy and now they were angry, as well. They drove through the line with vicious off-tackle thrusts and gained around the ends behind burly interference.

Only when they got inside the twenty-yard line, Cedar Creek's resistance stiffened like a wall. The first downs were no longer easy to get. Chauncey Dale dropped back to try a pass.

Perhaps there was some luck in the fact that the ball came to the right—the side Russ Green defended. Right in front of him he saw the Paxton end cut in to take the pass, but a leaping stride got him there first. His outstretched fingers gripped the leather, and momentum carried him straight ahead. It was the sort of thing he had done a thousand times that summer in the pasture. And the tangle of sprawled bodies in front of him—the clutching arms of tacklers caught off balance—were no harder to dodge than the boulders and juniper bushes up by Big Baldy.

In a moment he was past them and the white lines were flashing by under his feet. There was a swift thud of pursuit, but out of the corner of his eye he saw Jim Lowden cut behind him like a whirlwind, and the sound of running feet stopped. Then he was pounding on toward the last chalk-line, his breath coming in labored gasps. He could hear them gaining on him. As he crossed the five-yard stripe a diving tackler caught him around the knees, but the hurtling fall carried him over with a foot to spare.

They tried kicking the extra point and missed. Score 13-0, with the game only ten minutes old.

From then till the end of the half it was a dog-fight. At first the big red-shirted team played savagely but loosely. The sting of that second touchdown had spoiled their timing. Signals were missed. Plays were bungled. But they kept moving down the field by sheer power. Twice they marched fifty or sixty yards, only to lose the ball on backfield fumbles, and each time Russ Green was forced to kick out of danger. Then, in the final minutes of the half, Paxton began clicking. Replacements had come in, and the new men looked even bigger to the tired Cedar Creek line.

"That's the third heavyweight they've sicked on me," panted Bob Lewis to his side-kick, Evans. "Next guard they put in'll be a five-ton truck, I bet!"

They were making a dogged stand again, back on their three-yard line. A power-smash at tackle pushed them back a yard. Beany Singer ripped through the interference to stop an end run without gain. With two yards to go on last down, Paxton tried a spinner through center. The massed defense gave grudgingly under the impact. But when the whistle had blown and the pile was untangled, the ball was still short of the goal-line by inches. A few seconds later the half ended.

Back in the field-house Wickham did what he could to make the boys forget their weariness. He went the rounds, rubbing the worst of the bumps with liniment and applying bandages where they were needed. Meanwhile he kept up a running fire of cheerful talk.

"Sure," he told them. "They've got the weight and the substitutes. But remember—they're town boys. They haven't got the stuff inside—the toughness that's built up by plowing and cutting wood and pitching hay. They can't take it for sixty minutes. And you can!"

He slapped the stopper into the liniment bottle and

grinned at them all. "First downs?" he said scornfully. "They must have made fifteen or twenty. But we don't pay off on first downs in this man's game. Let 'em get tired running up and down the field! We'll do our fighting on the goal-line. Well, boys, it's time to go out."

They weren't cocky when they returned to the scene of conflict. They knew that thirteen-point lead would make the going all the rougher. But they meant to hold it just the same.

Two minutes after the kick-off Paxton had the ball and was rolling up first downs again. They must have been given a going-over between the halves, for there was an added bitterness in their charging and blocking. It also appeared that they were out to get Cedar Creek's goat. Every time one of their big linemen slammed into a guard or tackle, he would follow up with a jibe. "How ya like that, cowboy?"—or "Guess the old pasture was never like this!"

Occasionally, down under the scrimmage, a fist would be used on some unprotected spot. But this was poor strategy, as it turned out. Arne and Ole Nelson—the two big "plow-oxen" on the right side of the line—had been playing their usual game. They were slow, good-natured, tireless, but never spectacular. All of a sudden, Ole saw his brother's nose dripping red when they staggered up after a play. His blue eyes went steely. "Ay bane get that guy," he muttered. And the ferocity of his next charge laid the Paxton tackle out with a cracked rib. There were few gains made through the Swedes' sector of the line after that.

Desperately tired from the hammering they were taking, the green-shirts found themselves making another last-ditch stand before ten minutes had passed. Bang—bang at the line, and the ball reached the one-yard mark. Then a power-swing around right end, with four galloping interferers. Chick Harrison went down fighting under the avalanche, and Russ Green, backing him up, was overwhelmed before he could get his hands on the runner. Paxton had a touchdown.

Chauncey Dale, who was an artist at place-kicking, converted the extra point with ease.

The town rooters had plenty of confidence as the final quarter started. They knew it was just a matter of time now. Fresh replacements had come in and the steam roller looked irresistible. Up in the stands the steady clank of cow-bells sounded a dirge for Cedar Creek.

Two grim rallies in the shadow of the goal-posts succeeded in holding the red machine for downs as the minutes dragged by. A break came the lighter team's way when Paxton fumbled and Goat Walker recovered.

Green's long punt set the attackers back sixty yards, and they had to start all over again.

But the third down-field march couldn't be stopped. Big Joe Stein crashed a hole between Lewis and Evans and a Paxton line-plunger dove through into touch-down territory. A minute later the ball sailed in a low arc from Dale's toe, struck the cross-bar, hesitated a moment—and dropped back into the scrimmage. No goal. The score stood 13-13.

Russ Green called for time out. "Listen," he said hoarsely to the panting, sweat-stained crew around the water-bucket. "Maybe we can hold 'em. If a tie is all you fellows want, we'll try for a tie. What about it?"

Red-headed Goat Walker stood up, spitting out a mouthful of water. "The heck with that!" he croaked. "I'm through bein' a door-mat. Let's get that ball, an' forget about holdin' 'em!"

"Right!" came the muttered chorus. "We take it away from 'em, by yiminy!" growled the aroused Ole Nelson.

Green turned to the referee. "How much time?" he asked.

"Minute and a half. You're kicking off to Paxton."

Russ spoke to the ends as he went out to tee-up the ball. "Get down there fast and over to the right," he said. He set the oval carefully on its mound of earth and stepped back. With the whistle the ball flew end over end, swift, low and toward the corner. The Paxton back waited for it to go over the line, but after a couple of crazy bounces it rolled back, dead, on the five-yard stripe. Hastily he picked it up, only to find his legs locked fast in Beany Singer's arms.

"Hold 'em now—make 'em kick!" whispered Peewee Gates, slapping the sweat-darkened rumps of the crouching linemen. And their lunging fury smeared the first play before it could start.

Chauncey Dale dropped back, far into the end zone. The two lines tensed for action. Big Arne Nelson looked into Joe Stein's scowling visage, two feet away, and his slow mind produced a gem of thought. He chuckled. "Iss fine cheer you give, up in cow-pasture," he said. "Wah-hoo! Wah-hoo!"

The black-haired tackler's jaw dropped. He stared at the Swede, disconcerted. And then, as the ball was snapped, big Arne charged. He was no ox now, but a raging tiger. His mighty spring upset the Paxton captain and carried him deep into the enemy backfield. Leaping as high as he could, he stopped the ball's bullet-like rise with his huge hands and—miraculously—held on to it. There he stood, across the goal-line, his grinning, blood-smeared face a crimson flag of victory.

The Paxton team lined up listlessly to defend against the try for point. All their fight was gone. As the final whistle blew, Russ Green booted a perfect placement over the bar, and the game was ended. The figures on the score-board—above that taunting sign—read "Paxton, 13—Visitors, 20."

Cedar Creek came off the field. Slowly, too tired for jubilation, they pulled off their soaked uniforms and relaxed in the hot showers. Jack Wickham's voice came to them, exultant, through the steam.

"Outweighed fifteen pounds to the man!" he was saying. "And they were a hard bunch of bruisers, too! I can't figure yet how you boys did it."

Peewee Gates' shrill laugh answered him. "Maybe they were hard," the midget quarterback piped, "—but they weren't half as hard as some o' those trees an' rocks in Haley's pasture, were they, gang?"

ICE ON THE HORSE-KILLER

Horse-killer hill had borne its evil name for two hundred years. Jeff Morgan sometimes wondered which of his colonial ancestors had first put that appropriate name in circulation. Whoever had bestowed it, it had stuck.

Jeff, tramping with his sled up the ridge road that ran along the north crest, paused as he came to the intersection, and looked down the zigzag length of the famous hill.

Between the spot where he stood and Benham Village, two miles away, the road dropped a thousand feet. It had never been surfaced, for it was used only by the half dozen families whose farms lay along the ridge. And such cars as scaled its stony track toiled up in low gear.

Jeff's lanky red setter went ranging a hundred yards down the hill. There he swung and looked back, questioningly. The boy whistled.

"Not this trip, Pat," he grinned. "Thought you'd race me down, eh? Wait till the coasting's better. Then when Wink and I get our bob finished, you'll see some real speed!"

Wink Berry lived on the next farm. When Jeff reached the dooryard, his chum was just coming out of the barn.

"Hi, old-timer," called Wink. "Chores done already? You must've got up early."

"I did," Jeff answered. "What made you so slow?"

"Just luxury," the other boy laughed. "Christmas vacation only comes once a year, an' Pa let me lie abed till 'most six. I'm all done now, though, and it's only ten-thirty. We ought to finish her up today. Did you bring that auger bit?"

Jeff fished it out of his mackinaw pocket. "Right here," he answered. "Three-quarter-inch size. And Dad got me the bolts last night."

"Swell!" said Wink. "Let's get goin'."

They made for the Berry's carpenter shop. On the bench lay a plank of clear white pine, eight feet long and fourteen inches wide. Originally it had been two inches in thickness, but hours of careful planing had reduced it to an inch and a half.

Now Jeff set the plank edgewise in the vise and picked up a draw-knife. "I'll round off her stern while you're putting the rockers on the sleds," he said.

Wink brought the two sleds together and looked at them proudly. One was Jeff's and the other his own.

They had built them the year before, and had them shod with spring steel rods.

"Let's see," Wink mused. "Which did we decide was the fastest?" He looked at Jeff comically, with one eye closed—the expression that had given him his nickname.

Jeff laughed. "You know dog-gone well which," he said. "I beat you by ten yards every time we raced."

"Hm, maybe you're right," Wink nodded. "But mine's a little the solidest. I was just figurin' which to put in front."

"Well," Jeff chuckled, "your sled must feel sort of at home lookin' at mine from behind. I doubt if she'd know how to act up front. Besides, you say she's solider and there's generally more weight on the rear."

Wink gave his sled a comforting pat. "Never mind, old girl," he said. "We'll overlook his insults. Under the rear you go." With that he proceeded to screw a cross rocker of ash solidly on to the middle of the sled seat. Two holes were bored through the rocker, ready for the double eyebolts that were to hinge the board to the sled. A similar block of ash was fastened to Jeff's racer, and a single three-quarter-inch hole sunk through its center. This was to take the heavy kingbolt on which the steering sled would pivot.

When Jeff had finished his work on the plank, the

upper rockers were made fast to its under side. By noon they had the bob ready to assemble.

A cow horn sounded its mellow note from the house. "Gosh!" murmured Jeff. "Dinner time! I'll have to be hiking."

"Hold on!" said Wink. "You're stayin' here. Mom said so."

Jeff was not in the least unwilling. They called his home on the jingling farm-line telephone, then washed and went in to the table. Half an hour later, filled with Mrs. Berry's excellent cooking, they returned to the shop.

"Not so fancy to look at," Jeff admitted, as he stood over their handiwork. "But I bet she'll travel."

"Say," Wink exclaimed, "did you hear about the swell new bob Bert Mallet got for Christmas? Pa says it cost $300. It's got foot rests and handrails and brakes and springs, and a real steering wheel like an auto!"

Jeff whistled. "Sounds like one o' those Olympic sleds!" he said. "Wonder if Bert'll bring it up on the Horse-killer?"

Bert Mallet was the son of Benham's richest citizen —president of the bank and owner of the paper mill. Bert led the wealthy high school clique.

"Hope he does come up," Wink grinned. "He'll wear some o' the gilt paint off on those turns."

In another hour the big sled was completed—with final touches in the shape of a carefully notched foot brace across the forward end of the seat and a new steering rope of stout half-inch manila.

Then the two boys stood back to admire their job.

"Long enough to hold four," remarked Jeff at last, "and that's all we want. Low enough to keep right side up on the curves. Light enough to pull uphill, but still good and strong. She's built for these hills. I'm proud of her, Wink."

"Right," Wink nodded. "Now all we need is some more snow!"

.   .   .   .

Snow was not long in coming. It was the following night, as Jeff crossed the barnyard carrying his two pails of milk, that he felt the chill, furry touch of the flakes on his cheek. The sky was black and starless, and a north wind came wailing out of the pasture pines. It snowed steadily all that night, and there was no leaving the farm next day. Just before dusk, however, the village plow came through to open the road. It was a sturdy tractor of the caterpillar type, and pushed aside a ten-foot swath of snow as it worked its way up along the ridge. Not until the road to the last farm was broken out did the plow swing back and go roaring away, down Horse-killer Hill.

There was some traffic over the roads during the next three days, and New Year's Eve found the hill in the best condition of the winter. Jeff and Wink had tried out their new bob once or twice and were more than satisfied with its performance.

After supper that evening, the Morgans' telephone rang. Wink was on the other end of the wire.

"There'll be a moon tonight," he announced. "And I hear two or three sleds are comin' up from the village. How about some coasting?"

"Sure, I can go," said Jeff. "Who else shall we get?"

"I'll call up the Stover twins," came Wink's reply. "Be here in half an hour."

The night was cold and still, and as Jeff left the house he saw the white half-disc of a young moon riding high in the south. Pat, the big red setter, whined and scratched inside the shed door, and after a moment's hesitation the boy let him out.

"Come on, then, night-hound," he laughed, "but don't sing at the moon. You've got to act respectable for these town folks."

They went up the white road together, Jeff in a straight line and Pat in frisking circles. At Wink's, the Stovers were already on hand—chunky young Johnny and his round-faced twin sister, Elsie.

"We're goin' to ride on your new sled," chuckled

Johnny. "Ought to make swell ballast! Huh-huh!" His voice was changing and the laugh ended in a squeak.

Jeff nodded. "Just so you kids keep your nerve, and lean when we tell you on the turns, we won't take anybody's dust," he said.

As they walked along the road, four abreast, pulling the new bob, there was a gleam of headlights down the ridge. Two cars had stopped at the top of Horse-killer Hill, and a sound of laughing voices came from them.

"That's Bert Mallet's crowd," said Elsie breathlessly. "Are you really goin' to race him down, Jeff?"

"The only way to race bobsleds is to see which goes the farthest at the bottom," Jeff explained. "Either that or time 'em, the way they do in the big races. You can't start together on a hill like this. There'd be a smash sure."

A party of eight young people was gathered beside the cars, and two long sleds gleamed in the moonlight. As Jeff's quartet drew near, one or two of the town boys spoke perfunctorily. Jeff and Wink strolled over to the Mallet bob.

"Hi, Bert," said Wink. "Hear you've got a new sled. Boy! She's a beauty, isn't she?"

The banker's son gave them a casual nod and continued his conversation with one of the girls. Jeff and

Wink, unembarrassed, went on examining the sled. It was low and wide, with a cushioned seat and steel footrests spaced at intervals inside the handrails. The big steering wheel was set back at a rakish angle under a metal cowl. And the whole affair was painted a glossy black, with gold arrows along each side.

"Oh, I say, Del—" came young Mallet's amused voice. "Look at this thing! Would you believe it?"

He was talking to the doctor's daughter, Adelaide Morrison, and pointing his fur mitten at the Morgan-Berry sled. Adelaide looked uncomfortable.

"I think it's fine," she said. "It looks strong—and fast, too. Did you make it yourself, Jeff?"

"Wink and I," answered Jeff gruffly. "Come on, Stovers—let's try the slide. You want to steer, Wink?"

They pulled the sled to the brow of the hill. Wink braced his feet on the crossbar and took a turn around each hand with the steering rope. Johnny Stover sat next behind him, his legs thrust out on either side. Next came Elsie, and a three-foot section of the plank was left for Jeff. "All set?" he called. "Here goes!"

He leaned with both hands on the tail of the bob and pushed it into motion. With a final shove, he vaulted into his seat and they were off.

For a quarter of a mile the road was straight as a plumb line, and steep as the roof of a house. They shot downward through a whistle of wind that made them gasp for breath. Then came the first turn, a sharp angle to the right.

"Lean!" yelled Wink and Jeff together.

All four of them swayed toward the inside of the curve, and the sled swept around in a flurry of snow. Fifty yards and then back to the left. "Lean!" came the shout, and again they swayed in rhythm.

"Whoopee!" howled Jeff as they straightened out on the long stretch of the lower hill.

The sled had taken the last turn at thirty miles an hour, and now it picked up speed steadily, whizzing down the smooth track like a rocket.

Jeff leaned forward. "Hold hard!" he called. "Here come the bumps!"

The bob went off the crest of a brief level place in the road and landed twenty feet farther down with a thrilling jolt that scarcely diminished its speed. Another leap followed and then a third. The sled rocked like a speed boat in a swell, but Wink held her nose straight and away they flew, down a gradually flattening grade. Their pace slackened on the valley floor, but they had enough momentum to carry them up a gentle rise and almost to the bridge that marked the beginning of the village.

"Boy, that's what I call coastin'!" Wink exulted. "Come on—let's get up there and have another!"

They began the long tramp up the hill and just as they reached the bumps Pat came tearing down to meet them, barking eagerly. At that moment a piercing siren blast sounded from above.

"Out o' the way!" panted Jeff. "Here comes Bert!"

They jerked the homemade bob to the right of the track, just in time. Over the top of the last bump the black sled came like a swooping hawk. A high-pitched sound of girls' voices rose to a scream as it passed.

They had climbed only a few steps farther when the other sled flew past, and five minutes later it was followed by one of the cars, grinding down in second gear.

"Come on," Jeff muttered. "They'll get hauled up and have two or three slides to our one if we don't hurry."

The car, packed with boys and girls and towing the two sleds, passed them a quarter of a mile from the top. But to their surprise neither bob descended again before they reached the summit.

Bert Mallet was apparently waiting for them. "We saw where you turned around," he called gloatingly. "Passed you by a hundred feet. We were clear up on the bridge before we stopped."

"Good goin'!" replied Wink, unperturbed. "Maybe we'll do better next time. Want to go first?"

"No," said Bert. "We'll be following you close, though." And he and his passengers took their places.

"My turn to steer," murmured Jeff. "And look out they don't run over you on the take-off, Wink. I reckon they're goin' to try to pass us."

Wink snorted.

"Run over me? They won't be in sight when I swing on!"

Jeff settled himself, and the Stovers got on behind him. Then, with a whoop, Wink started his push. Running his hardest for nearly thirty yards, he made a superhuman jump for the tail seat, and Jeff felt the solid thud of his landing give added impetus to the flying sled.

Suddenly, right at Jeff's elbow, a dark shape appeared —the big setter, trying to race with his master.

"Keep away, Pat!" he yelled. "Go home, you idiot! Want to get hit?"

The dog dropped back, already outspeeded by the sled. And in the same instant Mallet's siren blew frantically, just behind.

"They're comin'—right on top of us!" Johnny Stover howled in Jeff's ear. "Gosh—they 'most hit the pup!"

Jeff gritted his teeth with rage, but he dared not

take his eyes from the track ahead. Down they shot dizzily into the first turn and—"Lean!" he bellowed.

He held the bob to the hard snow in the middle of the road, and made the curve without slowing. Momentarily he expected to hear that siren again, and see the black sled creeping past. Probably it *was* faster. But he wasn't being beaten if he could help it.

Here came the second turn. "Lean!" and around they sped. Then down, down to the waiting bumps. They cleared them safely and still there was no sign or sound of their rivals. The sled skimmed across the level bottoms and started up the slope to the bridge. Slower and slower it moved. There was the ironwork alongside! Under them the hollow rumble of the snow-covered planks! And the bob eased to a stop.

"Let's see 'em beat that!" Wink howled with glee.

They looked back and saw the other sled gliding to a halt fifty yards behind them.

When they got back to it, Bert Mallet met them livid with anger. "It was that confounded dog of yours!" he stormed. "Got right in front of me and I had to steer into the edge of the drifts. Served him right if I'd hit him. Even then I came pretty near passing you. Didn't want to go by on that narrow road—"

"A good time to think of that," said Jeff, steadily, "would have been before you pushed off in such a hurry. Anybody that's coasted as much as you ought to know it's dangerous to run sleds that close together."

"Huh!" Mallet sneered. "Scared, are you? I'll run my bob as close as I please, and I'm going to prove I can pass you. What have you got to say about that?"

Wink's fists doubled and his eyes flashed, but Jeff's reply was in the same even tone. "If you want to act that way," he said, "I guess we'll just stay off the hill until you're through."

"Boys—please don't fight about it," Adelaide begged. "Go ahead and coast, Jeff. Bert won't bother you!"

Jeff elbowed Wink away and the party from the ridge set off with their sled.

"For two bits—" Wink growled, but Jeff interrupted him.

"I know," said he. "Bert was asking for it, but it wasn't the time. If he'd hit Pat, though—"

The rest of the evening passed without further conflict. They got in two more slides before bedtime, and took care to start when the others were down the hill. But the hostility between the boys and Bert Mallet did not end that night.

Two days later school started, and that first morning Jeff found Bert Mallet setting forth the coasting situation to a knot of boys gathered by the coat rack.

"Naw," Mallet was saying scornfully, in a voice

raised for Jeff's benefit. "They wouldn't race. Guess they knew my sled would show 'em up."

Jeff shouldered deliberately into the circle. "Is that what you've been telling around town?" he asked. "You know mighty well we proved our bob could travel as far as yours. And nobody but a born fool would think of racing two sleds down the Horse-killer together. I'll take as many chances as you, any day, but I won't take 'em just to show off. It's got to be for something worth while."

"Yeah?" Mallet replied. "How much do you call worth while? Say five dollars? Or haven't you got that much?"

"I didn't expect you to understand," said Jeff indifferently, and turned on his heel.

Wink was furious when he heard about the conversation. "Gosh," he cried, "why didn't you let him have it right then?"

"I figure there'll be better ways to prove he's a liar," Jeff grinned. "I'll wait till they come along."

．　　．　　．　　．　　．　　．　　．

There was no more coasting that week. Two days of warm weather softened the snow. Then followed a day of heavy rain. It cleared off cold on Sunday and the mercury fell steadily till it was well below the zero mark. The snow in the fields was so thickly crusted it would bear a man's weight, and the long, steep track of Horse-killer Hill was sheeted with solid ice.

A big hay meadow lay back of Berrys' barn, and here Jeff and Wink tried out their sled on the crust. They found the sloping, icy surface lightning fast.

On Monday morning Jeff caught up with Bert Mallet on the school steps. Two or three of the town boy's friends were with him and they watched the pair expectantly. But Jeff was not picking a fight.

"Say, Bert," he remarked, "there's a swell crust up on the ridge. If you want to race bobsleds, this is your chance. Plenty of room for two or three abreast."

Mallet scowled. "We might come up," said he, "but a gang of us were going to the movies tonight, and—"

Jeff turned away coolly. "Oh, well," he smiled, "if you're not anxious to try it, that's your affair. You were doing a good deal of talking, you know. The moon's just past full tonight, and there may not be another good crust this winter."

Bert saw the eyes of his friends upon him. "Daring me, are you?" he flared. "Sure, we'll come!"

"Good enough," said Jeff heartily. "Ought to be fun. We'll have a bonfire, because it's going to be mighty cold. Your car'll have to come up around the end of the ridge, you know. The Horse-killer's ice from top to bottom."

At eight o'clock that night, just as the moon rose out of the eastern pines, the crowd from Benham Village arrived. Mr. Mallet's big car was towing the two bobs. He left the party beside the fire and drove on, telling them he would return about eleven.

Bert and his sled crew tried the hayfield crust several times and found plenty of thrills in its speed. After half an hour the banker's son called to Jeff.

"Hey, Morgan!" he said. "How about a little competition? We can line up all three sleds right here and start together."

Jeff was over by the fire. "Be ready in a jiffy," he answered. "I'm heating up some cocoa here for the crowd." He put more wood on the blaze under the big kettle, and ran back to the sleds.

There was no particular choice of positions. Wink pulled the homemade bob out to the right.

Bert Mallet was in the middle, at the wheel of his sled. "Ready?" he shouted. "I'll give a signal—'One—two—three—go!' And no starting before the word 'go'!"

Jeff took his place at the stern of the sled. Slowly Bert counted till he came to "three"; then instantly yelled, "Go!" His pusher, prepared for the trick, plunged into motion a full stride ahead of the others, but Jeff made it up in a swift rush before he jumped for the sled.

The homemade bob and the black one flashed down the first pitch on even terms, with the other town sled several lengths in the rear. Then for a hundred yards the slope became more gradual, and Mallet's smooth-running flyer crept slightly ahead.

The girls in both sled crews were screaming with excitement, and now Bert gave a yell of triumph. But the race wasn't over yet. Directly in front of the black bob a hummock appeared. And in his effort to steer around it, the town boy slewed sidewise on the icy crust. Wink, holding his course straight, shot into the lead and kept it. When the sleds stopped at the far side of the meadow, three or four lengths separated the two leaders, and the third bob was still farther behind.

Jeff found Bert Mallet sullenly engrossed in turning his sled.

"Tough luck," said the hill boy. "We won't count that one. You were ahead until you came to that hump."

Mallet looked up in surprise. "No," he said, grudgingly. "You won that heat. But we'll make it two out of three."

"Fair enough," replied Jeff. "Only let's have some cocoa first. It'll be good and hot by now."

With the temperature close to zero, the heat of the

big fire was welcome. The crowd gathered around it, chatting gaily, and pulling off their mittens to stretch their hands to the warmth.

Adelaide Morrison picked up a stick and stepped close to lay it on the blaze. As she thrust it forward, the end struck the lower edge of the cocoa kettle, and a sudden deluge of the scalding liquid drenched her hand and arm. With a stifled scream she stumbled back, white-faced, fighting the pain.

Jeff sprang to her side, pulling the bobsled. "Here—sit down on this," he ordered. "That's a nasty scald. The first thing to do is get some grease on it. Elsie! Bring me those sandwiches, quick."

He opened two or three sandwiches and snatched from them generous lumps of butter. "All right, Adelaide," he said. "This'll take some of the pain out."

She winced at his touch but made no outcry. As gently as he could, he rubbed the butter on her reddened wrist and hand.

"Listen," he said, "would your father—would Dr. Morrison be at home now?"

"Yes," she groaned, "but his office hours are over at nine and he'll be leaving in a few minutes."

Jeff stood up, and stared down Horse-killer Hill at the winking lights of the village. "We could phone," he said thoughtfully, "but it would take him too long

WINK SHOT INTO THE LEAD

to get here—round by the ridge. A thing like this needs attention quick."

Suddenly he turned to Wink Berry. "Wink," he said, "I think I can steer the Horse-killer. Are you game to go down? We could get her to her father's office in no time that way."

"Yes," answered Wink, "I'll go. What about it, Adelaide?"

"What!" Bert Mallet interrupted. "Why, you're crazy! With that ice? I tell you I wouldn't go down there for a million dollars!"

"Nobody expected you would," said Wink, coldly. "Want to go, Adelaide?"

She managed a smile. "I think I'd better," she said. "I know Father always says burns ought to be dressed quickly. And I'm not scared—much."

"Come on," said Jeff, and pulled the sled into the road. Wink and the girl followed, and the rest straggled after them in silence. In a moment the homemade bob was ready at the top of the hill. Jeff looked at the sky and was thankful to see no clouds near the moon. He would need its light. With his feet on the brace, and his mittens wrapped in the steering rope, he glanced over his shoulder.

"All set, Adelaide?" he asked. "Wink'll help you stay on. Not much run, Wink—just enough to start us."

The other boy pushed the sled slowly into motion and settled into his place at the rear.

"Hang on with one hand," he told the girl. "I'll hold you when we have to lean."

From the gentle glide of its start, the bob picked up speed incredibly, second by second. The steel runners clicked and whined down the slanted plane of glassy ice.

Jeff choked back a spasm of fear and gripped his ropes hard. It was so much faster than any ride he had ever known. He felt so powerless to control the falling thing under him. The wind drove straight into his eyes— whirled the breath out of his throat.

Here it came—the turn—rushing to meet him. There were frozen ruts in the road, and he had kept out of them till now. But in a flash he knew they were his salvation. Desperately he steered across the left-hand rut and let the right runners drop into it, banking the sled inward just as they struck the turn. "Lean!" he cried.

The narrow trough of ice held the bob true—kept them from skidding off into the brush and rocks that lined the road. Jeff had a fleeting glimpse of a shallow place in the rut ahead. As they flashed down to it, he gave a mighty jerk to the right, and brought the front sled out. The bob was honestly built and the rear runner trailed straight—jumped the rut obediently in the track of its leader. At the start of the second curve, Jeff eased the left side of the sled into the trough, and again, as they swayed inward, the grip of the ice held them on the road.

They were around, and straightening away for the lower hill, but now a new danger threatened. The sled was still canted to the left—still riding the rut—and no opportunity came to release it.

"Keep leaning!" yelled Jeff, and they leaned, holding the bob from going over by the sheer weight of their bodies. So for twenty dizzy, swaying seconds, they rocketed down the frozen track. Not till the first bump did Jeff find his chance. There, in the brief level before the crest, the ruts gave way to a smooth sheet of ice. The sled skimmed across it and sailed outward, to land in the middle of the road below, straight on its course.

Safely over the next bump, and the next, they flew —and down to the flat reaches of the valley floor. It was here, even more than on the hill, that they realized the terrific speed the ice gave them. Trees and fences fled past without apparent slackening. The rise to the bridge came and fell behind. They shot across the span and into the bright lights of Main Street. And twenty feet from Dr. Morrison's door they finally came to a stop.

Bert Mallet was waiting for Jeff Morgan at the school entrance next morning. His face wore an embarrassed grin.

"Say, Jeff," he began gruffly, "I want—I'd like—well, you know how I feel. You've got nerve all right—got it when it counts! Doc Morrison says you saved Adelaide a bad scar—maybe saved her hand. And—I'll take off my hat to that sled of yours. I'll back you up any time you want to claim the championship of Horse-killer Hill!"

THE WILL TO WIN

WINFIELD SCOTT HADDON, red-headed and eighteen, sat alone on the bench in front of his locker and fought the nervousness that always attacked him before a race. There was still half an hour before the 880 would be called. It was a mild May Saturday, far from chilly, but Haddon shivered. He reached down to pull on his sweat-pants and saw the muscles in his long white legs trembling.

It was silly. This would be his third dual meet as a Varsity track man, and he was behaving like a stage-struck novice.

A door slammed and the voice of a distracted assistant manager echoed through the gymnasium.

"Hey—Win!"

"I'm coming," answered Haddon in a tone he tried to make gruff and casual. "What's the matter?"

"Coach wants you on deck," panted the courier. His flushed, bespectacled face appeared in the locker-room door. There was something about Boob Belton's face that always provoked laughter. He was like a figure out of a comic cartoon.

"What's that slung around your neck, Boob?" Haddon asked with a chuckle.

"Movie camera," the other replied. "I got to hurry back or I'll miss the quarter. Takin' pictures of all the races at the finish line. Shake a leg!"

Win pulled on his sweat shirt and followed at a slower pace. The spring sun warmed his back. His legs began to feel as if they belonged to him once more. He flexed his knees in a few high-prancing strides and crossed the track to join the group around the high-jump pit. There was no stadium at Cameron College. Just a wooden grandstand, in which a few hundred students and townspeople now sat, and the field, dotted with athletes.

Pop Hamilton, veteran coach, turned his grizzled head and nodded.

"Feel good, Haddon?" he asked.

"Sure—fine," Win answered. "How do we stand, Coach?"

"Pretty even," Pop frowned. "We've got 37 points and Harley has 35, with six events to go. They're sure in the two-mile and the discus. We've got a possible edge in the high hurdles and broad jump. Pole vault's a toss-up. If we can get our first and second in the half, we may win. It's up to you and Deak. Go over there with him and limber up."

On the turf by the straightaway, Deak Dennison was jogging in long strides, reaching out with his spikes. To young Haddon he was everything a hero should be. Cameron's track captain and first-string half-miler— a senior, big, handsome, hard-working, with a mature face and a determined jaw.

Deak greeted him with a grin. "Collywobbles all gone, kid?" he asked. "That's good. We'll show 'em today. Chalk up eight points for Cameron."

The pair took some practice starts and trotted up and down the turf.

"First call for the 880!" shouted the announcer, and they began peeling off their warm-up garments.

"Pop wants you to set the pace, today," Dennison whispered. "Step right out and run. Harley has one man in the race that's pretty good. The other's a second-rater. I'll stay with their best man and watch him. Maybe you'll be able to pull him out so he won't have any sprint left."

Haddon nodded his understanding. As they walked across to the starting line he looked up at his captain. "This is your last dual meet for Cameron, isn't it? I bet you hate the idea."

"Yep," Deak replied, laughing. "No letter for me this year if I don't win today. One more five-pointer is all I need."

They took their places. A short, thick-muscled Harley man had the pole. Deak gave Win a nudge. "He's the one," he whispered.

The two Cameron runners had second and third positions, with Win inside. As they stood there waiting for the word to take their marks, Deak gave Win a final smile of encouragement and held out his hand.

"Here's one we take!" said he.

"First and second!" replied the redhead. It was their regular ritual—not simply an offering to Lady Luck but a last-minute stiffener of morale.

"On your marks," called the starter, pointing his pistol at the cinders. "Get set." *Bang!*

Win got away fast—shoulder to shoulder with the chunky Harley man for the first few yards. Then he quickened his stride, shot ahead, cutting over strongly to take the pole. With a surge of action, his tenseness fell away like a cloak. He seemed loose-limbed and free and filled with limitless power. It was the first time he had ever run in front. He wondered if the pace was too fast—he had rounded the first turn at a 440 clip. But he felt strong. His wind was good. And he settled down to a long, even stride as he sailed up the back stretch.

There was a quick, steady pounding of feet behind him. That would be the Harley runner. Deak's steps, he knew, were longer. Win let out a notch and scorched around the upper turn with the patter of feet growing fainter in the rear.

At the head of the straightaway he felt his first discomfort. There was a tightness in his chest. It was difficult to get enough air. All right—nothing to do but plow ahead and wait for his second wind. It came with a rush—a grateful coolness in his throat—a loosening of the bonds that had clutched his ribs. He breathed quicker, in rhythm with his stride, and once more he was running easily and fast.

The first lap was done. A babel of encouraging yells from teammates and spectators followed him as he swung again into the lower curve. He wouldn't look back—yet. He knew his job was to keep up the pace as long as he could—scare his rival into making an early sprint. And so he ran, still strong on the back-stretch, laboring a little on the last curve, definitely tiring as the track straightened out for the final struggle.

His head was ringing. His knees felt uncertain. It was increasingly hard to get his breath. Down the interminable home stretch he pounded, with the track rocking under him like the deck of a ship. Fifty yards more. Time for Deak to come flying by in that famous driving finish of his.

Dimly, through the drumming of blood in his ears,

he heard the thud of feet behind. He still had something left. Instinct told him he could win if he would, and the temptation was strong. But he remembered in time what his captain had said—"one more five-pointer." Deak's last college letter! No, Deak must win.

With twenty yards to go, Haddon turned his head —saw another white jersey two steps behind. He stumbled, lost his stride, caught his balance again just as the other passed. And then to his horror he realized that it wasn't Deak. There was the chunky Harley man ahead, wobbling on short, muscular legs but fighting forward to the tape.

Frantic, the redhead dashed after him. He gained. He flung himself at the taut white string in a last frenzied bound. But it didn't snap across his chest. Instead, its broken end floated away from him as he crossed the line.

The Harley man, winner by inches, staggered a few steps and fell on the sod beside the track, completely out. In his despair Win would have been glad to do the same. But he could still stand, looking blankly back along the cinder path. He saw Deak Dennison limp in, seconds later, with one foot bare. So that was it. Lost a shoe. Five priceless points to Harley! And there was Boob Belton, his comedy face fixed in an idiotic grin, still grinding mechanically away at his little movie camera.

Dazed by the catastrophe, Win watched Deak and the coach come toward him. There was distress in Pop Hamilton's eyes.

"You had that fellow licked, Win," he said. "Too bad! Just a little more drive at the end and we'd had that race. We need it, too. Harley won the pole vault."

The coach turned away and Win faced Deak. The captain's eyes were hard. "I always thought you were a fighter, Haddon," he said bitterly. "Guess I was mistaken."

"But, Deak—" Win began, then stopped abruptly. He knew that to spectators it must have seemed that he had quit. That instant of faltering when his rival threatened—that must have looked bad.

Deak had swung on his heel and was limping away. A sudden flare of the temper that matched his hair swept Win Haddon. Deak ought to know he hadn't quit! Flushed with anger, he started after his hero. He laid a hand on Deak's arm, and his voice was husky as he spoke.

"Listen to me!" he said. "When I was halfway down the stretch—"

"Alibis don't interest me," the captain replied coldly. He pulled his arm away and walked off.

Win looked blankly after him, turned without a word, and picked up his sweat clothes. In the gym he took a shower, dressed, and slammed shut the door of his locker with a gesture of finality that went with his black mood. He was done with track. Done with sacrifice. From now on whatever he did would be done for one person—himself.

.   .   .   .

The Cameron *Chronicle* was the student newspaper, issued weekly. At four o'clock on Monday, Win Haddon came back from a lab period in sophomore chemistry and found the paper tucked under his door. Listlessly he picked it up and glanced at the headlines. There was a full account of the Harley track meet— the first dual meet Cameron had lost in two years. Win swallowed hard and turned the page with a vicious sweep. His eye fell on an editorial. It was headed, "The Will to Win." After a rather high-flown opening paragraph, the undergraduate editor expressed himself as follows:

"On Saturday afternoon there was shown on Cameron Field an example of something utterly foreign to the true spirit of our college. A race that might have been won by a fighting finish was lost by the lack of it. What made the spectacle all the more distressing was the fact that the loser appeared strong after the line was crossed, while his rival collapsed after giving his all for victory. We can only suggest that nicknames are sometimes misleading."

Tears boiled up in Win's eyes and he slammed the paper on the floor. At that moment a knock sounded and Pop Hamilton entered the room. The kindly expression of his weathered face was lost on Win. To him the coach appeared only as a blurred outline.

"Hello, Red," said Pop, casually. "I looked for you out at the track. What's the matter?"

"You know well enough," Win choked. "I'm through with running. If it weren't for my dad, and the way he's worked to send me here, I'd be through with Cameron."

"Pshaw!" answered the coach. "Don't take it so hard. You ran a first-class race. All you need's experience. You'll know how to rate yourself along, next time."

His glance fell on the paper by Win's chair. "As for that silly piece in the *Chronicle*," he said, "forget it! The guy that wrote it never sweated his heart out in a race or he'd know better. And the college doesn't feel that way. We're counting on you to win points in the Conference meet Saturday. Come on and get the kinks out of your legs."

Win shook his head emphatically. "No," he replied. "I'm done, and I mean it."

Hamilton's face was incredulous. "You're going to let this lick you?" he asked. "You're going to quit under fire?"

"I'm going to mind my own business!" blazed the redhead.

The coach looked at him pityingly. "Well," he said, as he turned to go, "maybe you're not interested, but the time of that half mile, Saturday, was 1:59⅘—just two-fifths of a second over the Conference record. I wouldn't hang up my track suit when I was that close, if I were you."

In spite of himself, Win gasped as he heard the words. When the door had shut behind Hamilton, he slumped down on the bed, repeating them to himself. In that race he himself had touched the magic two-minute figure—the goal of every half-miler! He picked up the paper again and verified the time. There it was in black and white. For a moment he was keenly tempted to go out to the field. Then the editorial thrust its impish headline under his eyes and his rage flared up once more.

No, he would stay where he was—at least until Deak Dennison came and said he was sorry—for it was Deak's attitude that had hurt most. To the others it might have looked as if he'd quit. Deak ought to have known better.

But Deak didn't come that day, nor the next. Win was silent and sullen when he went to meals and classes. Two or three of his friends tried to argue him out of his mood, but their clumsy efforts only strengthened his decision. His sense of injustice weighed him down, and he was suspicious of every glance cast at him, every half-heard word.

By Wednesday afternoon he began to feel the lack of exercise. Surreptitiously he took his track shoes out of the locker, wrapped them in a newspaper, and plodded out of the campus by a back road. A mile away, in a quiet bit of country lane, he found a reasonably smooth stretch of earth, and there he put on the spiked shoes. For the best part of an hour, he jogged and sprinted and practiced starts.

It did him good. He felt more charitable toward the world, as he walked back—and a little ashamed of himself. Maybe tomorrow he would go out for regular practice.

The next noon as he was leaving the Commons after lunch, he saw a paper on the bulletin board, outside. It was a list of the track men who were to make the trip to Jonesville for the Conference meet on Saturday. Quickly Win's eye ran down the typewritten page. "880-yard run: Dennison, McCormick." That was all. McCormick—a second-string miler, who hadn't run an

880 in years! And the notice was signed, "J. D. Dennison, Capt."

Win stood it till his last class was over on Friday. Then he threw some clothes in a suitcase and started for the station. A huge poster on the gym door taunted him with its red-painted message: "Big Pep Meeting Tonight! Give the Track Team a Send-off! Win the Conference Title!"

He got aboard the 4:30 train for home and for an hour sat staring bitterly at the green May landscape. He hadn't written, and there was no one at the station to meet him; so he hiked the two miles up to the farm.

His mother was delighted when he appeared at the kitchen door, but her quick eye caught something behind his smile. "What's the matter, Son?" she asked when the greetings were over.

"Oh, nothing," he mumbled. "Just got homesick for a sight of you. Where's Dad? Is it milking time yet?" He ate supper, helped with the evening chores, and joined the family around the reading lamp.

"Hm," said his father, looking up from the paper, "I see there's a big track meet tomorrow, over at Jonesville. No team in it from Cameron?"

"Y-yes," said Win glumly. "They'll be there all right."

And then, before more questions were asked, "Guess I'll go to bed."

He rose and started for the stairs, but was stopped in the hall by the jingle of the telephone. A voice, faint but familiar, answered his "hello."

"Is that you, Haddon? Win, this is Deak Dennison. I just came out of that pep meeting, and I've got one big apology to make. How I could have been so confoundedly stupid, I don't know. But I thought you'd quit cold in that race, until I saw the movies. . . . What? Why the movies Boob Belton made. He ran 'em off on the screen tonight as part of the general hoo-raw. Showed the finish of all the runs. And when I saw you slow up and look back, it came to me like a flash what you were trying to do. Darn white of you, kid! By the time I got in, those cinder cuts on my foot were hurting so, I guess I talked rougher than I meant. At that, I was coming round to make my peace if the doc hadn't kept me bandaged up in the infirmary for three days."

"Gee, Deak," Win stammered into the transmitter, "I'm glad you don't think I folded up. I wouldn't blame you. I—I was sore too. I'm the one that's been a wall-eyed sap."

"Forget it!" laughed Deak. "Say, can you get over to Jonesville by ten tomorrow morning? You've got a car? Swell! The half mile trial heats are at ten-thirty.

And now I'm on my way to the *Chronicle* office to take the hide off that idiot of an editor! So long, old man."

Win's whoop of joy woke the venerable watch dog in the barn, and brought his father out of the living room on the run.

"What's happened?" asked Mr. Haddon.

"Everything!" cried the boy. "How far is it to Jonesville?"

"Ninety-five or a hundred miles. Why? Going there in a hurry? The car's in town, being overhauled."

Win's face fell. "Gosh!" said he. "There's no train, either. What about the old flivver?"

"It's jacked up in the hen house, where you left it last fall," his father replied. "But you'll never drive that to Jonesville!"

"Watch me!" said Win, grimly. "I'm going to run a race tomorrow, and nothing's going to stop me."

He yanked on a pair of overalls, lit a lantern, and went to work. Under the dust, the ancient vehicle still had most of its vital organs intact. It was a touring car, topless and with one door gone, but the engine had been the object of Win's affections for years. He drained the oil out of the cylinders, cleaned the spark plugs, fiddled with the points, wiped off the timer, greased a few necessary joints and bearings. Then he put oil in the crankcase and gas in the tank, filled the radiator, and tried to turn her over.

For long minutes he jerked at the crank furiously, pausing only to tinker with connections. No spark. The battery was dead, of course. Wiping away the sweat, he started pumping tires. One had a leak and he patched the tube. Behind the barn he found two discarded casings that he put in the rear seat for spares. And at 11:30, with an aching back and blisters on his hands, he climbed the stairs to bed.

The alarm clock woke him before dawn. His mother was already up and gave him breakfast. Luckily he had packed his track outfit in his suitcase, and he tossed it into the flivver. Then he took his place at the wheel and called his father from the barn.

"If you'll give her a push down the hill, Dad," he said, "I'll try to start her on the magneto."

Across the dew-spangled grass the old car rolled majestically, and down the driveway, heading into a pink sunrise. Midway of the hill she gave an explosive snort. An instant later all her hardware was rattling to the erratic roar of the engine. And Win was off for Jonesville.

That morning's ride was an epic in itself. He had two blowouts and a short circuit. His radiator leaked. He ran out of gas. And each time he stopped, it was necessary to beg a push from a passing car. But at precisely 10:22—almost six hours from home—the flivver limped down the main street of Jonesville and in at the gates of the State Agricultural College.

The coach and Deak Dennison were waiting outside the big drill hall where the visiting athletes had their dressing quarters. Deak sprang forward with a shout of relief.

"Just in time, boy!" he cried. "We've got you placed in the third qualifying heat; so you'll have another quarter of an hour to get out on the field. I've got to beat it, now. My heat's been called."

Win watched him jog away and saw that there was a little hitch in his step—a tight surgical bandage swathing one foot. Pop Hamilton frowned. "Deak's game," he said gruffly. "But it's you that's got to run today, Haddon. Get into those clothes, now."

Out at the track, Win got his instructions. A third place would put him in the finals, but the coach advised him to run to win.

"Everybody else'll be counting on taking it easy and just coming in third," he said. "Someone's sure to get left."

Deak Dennison's heat was just starting. The big Cameron captain showed no limp as he sped smoothly around at the heels of the leader. But on the second lap his face was drawn and his breathing labored. Another runner passed him to take second place, and only a desperate finish enabled him to qualify.

He leaned on Win's shoulder as he came off the track.

"Began to feel it on the back stretch, second time round," he panted between clenched teeth. "I'll get the doc to dress it again. Win—get in there and run!"

Win had warmed up, shaken the stiffness of the long drive out of his leg muscles. There were seven others beside himself in the heat, and he had the pole. At the gun, the man next him cut over in front with a violent effort, and set the pace for the first furlong. Then he dropped back and another challenged, but Win stayed in second place. On the last curve before the finish he found the leader's stride slackening, and sprinted around him to open up a ten-yard gap on the field. He was slowed down when he crossed the line, an easy winner—and the time was 2:02.

"Nice work," the coach nodded. "You didn't get tired. There are fast men in the final, though. That Harley chap won the first heat in two flat, and Deak's heat was only a shade over."

He looked at Win more closely. "There are circles under your eyes. Need sleep?"

"I only got about four hours last night," the boy admitted.

"All right," said Pop. "The Aggies' coach is a friend of mine. I'll get you fixed up."

Win drank some orange juice and beef tea, and was given a cot in a quiet wing of the gymnasium. The final of the half mile was scheduled for 5 P.M.—one of the last events of the meet. The boy slept soundly for two hours, then rested and dozed awhile, and by four he was out on the field again.

Cameron had so far won first in only a single event— the low hurdles. But Cameron men had placed all along the line, taking a few seconds and thirds and many fourths. As the time for Win's race approached, the scores stood: State Aggies, 27; Harley, 25; Cameron, 24—with the rest of the points strung out among the dozen colleges that formed the Conference.

Win trotted up and down nervously, the old chills creeping along his spine. Deak wasn't exercising. He sat still, favoring his injured foot, and his face was calm.

"I've got a two-minute race in me," he said, "but that won't win. If I can pull out a third or fourth, though, and you can take first—" he paused, searching Win's eyes with his own—"then we've got this meet won!"

On the starting line, the redhead looked across at

HE RAN LIKE A RED-HAIRED TYPHOON

his captain. He himself was in seventh position—Deak at No. 2. Deak made a gesture of shaking hands.

"Two places!" Win grinned in reply, and crouched.

In the swift scramble for the pole, Win was content to take fifth and hold it around the curve. Then he let out, running as he had at Cameron. He passed two men on the first straight stretch, and swung the upper turn at Deak's heels.

The leader of the pack was a long-legged runner wearing the colors of a small upstate college. He looked strong and he was steadily pulling away from the pack. Win had his second wind now. He gave the grim-faced Deak a smile and went ahead of him as they entered the last lap. Five yards behind at the beginning of the back stretch, he let out a notch, creeping closer. Then for the first time he heard behind him a quick thud of spikes. Flying up on the outside came a short, brawny figure— his old enemy, the Harley half-miler. And Win was boxed.

Around the final turn the trio sped, to a frenzied yelling from the stands. Then, sixty yards from home, the tall upstate boy began to stagger. Win had to check his speed to avoid running into him, and when he did get safely by, the Harley man had forged ahead to a lead that looked unbeatable.

To Win Haddon, pounding desperately along,

came a hunch: "This fellow thinks it's easy—thinks I'm a quitter!"

The word roweled him like a spur. He ran like a red-haired typhoon, closing the gap, yard by yard. He fought his way abreast, and for ten yards they battled elbow to elbow, chins thrust out and mouths twisted in effort. With the last stride Win lunged—and felt the tape break against his jersey.

A moment later Deak tumbled into Win's arms. "Six—points," he gasped. "It's Cameron's meet now—letters for all of us! And listen!"

"Time," an announcer was braying, "one fifty-nine and one-fifth. A new Conference record!"

CROOKED ARM

WHEN Bill Wingate made his first appearance at Riverdale High School, he was sixteen years old and six feet three in his shoepacks. He came rattling down from the mountain in an unbelievably ancient flivver, parked it with its nose to a tree, and ambled up the steps. His great red wrists hung far out of his coat sleeves. His neatly patched trousers missed his ankles by inches, and he wore an odd-looking little felt hat perched on his mop of sandy hair. But the most noticeable thing about him was his grin. It was so wide and friendly that even his grotesque length and outlandish costume were forgotten by the crowd of students who stood staring as he approached.

"Hi, folks," he nodded to them and went in.

Ten minutes later, in the principal's office, he registered as a sophomore. He had come to Riverdale High because, as he expressed it, he had "got all the education they could give" in the little frame school up on Hog Back.

When lunch time came he returned to the flivver and from somewhere in its rear hauled out a large newspaper package of sandwiches, doughnuts, and pie. As he sat on the running board munching his meal an informal welcoming committee strolled up. New boys were always objects of interest at Riverdale.

"Can you play football?" asked Joe Clark, a junior and a halfback.

Bill shook his head—and grinned.

"How about basketball?" put in diminutive Reddy Reynolds, manager of the court team. "You look as if you could jump center."

"No, I—I never even saw that game," stammered Bill, still grinning.

Big Ed Krusen winked at Clark. "Well, Shorty," he said, "you must be a star baseball player, then."

For the first time the expression on Bill's freckled face became serious. "Why, no," he said. "I wouldn't say I'm so good as that, but I've played some, up on Hog Back."

"What position?" asked Reddy, solemnly.

"Pitcher," Bill answered, flushing. "Leastways I used to pitch, only last year there wa'n't nobody could hold me, in our little school."

This appeared to be too much for Reynolds. He turned away and leaned on Joe Clark's bosom, his shoulders shaking. Krusen stuck an elbow in the smaller fellow's ribs.

"See here, Slim," he addressed Bill severely, "a talent like yours—I might almost say a *gift* like yours—deserves to be given an immediate trial. I've got the big mitt in my locker, also a mask. Too bad the chest protector isn't here, but I'll risk my life in a good cause. Soon as you finish your repast come out back to the diamond. We'll have time to let two or three batters look over your shoots before the bell rings."

So saying he took each of the others by the arm and started for the gym.

The word traveled fast, and a good-sized crowd was gathered around the athletic field when Bill appeared.

"Here he comes," someone yelled. "Come on, Big Boy, show us some pitchin'!"

Bill looked around, hesitating. "Well—I—" he began.

"Come on," said Ed Krusen, standing behind the plate. "We'll just have time for a little game before classes."

The boy from Hog Back took off his out-grown jacket and laid it carefully on the ground. "Whar's the ball?" he asked.

"Here," said Joe Clark—"and you can have my glove." He came nearer, dropping his voice. "Don't let 'em kid you, boy," he said.

In a moment Bill found himself very much alone in the middle of the diamond. He looked with curiosity at the neat mound, the slab, and the worn foot holes. Krusen had donned the mask and mitt and was pounding a deep cup in the leather.

"Toss a couple," said he, and the mountain lad obediently tossed the ball, underhand, to the great amusement of the crowd. Krusen laughed with the rest. "All right, Lengthy, let her come!" he shouted as he snapped the ball back neatly into Bill's awkward hands.

The elongated pitcher set the ball down, took the glove off his left hand and worked it on to his right, jamming his big thumb into the little-finger hole. He grinned and looked around somewhat sheepishly at the boys.

"I—I'm a lefty," he said, as if admitting a secret vice.

The laughter grew at this, and rose in whoops and howls as Bill wound up. Beyond a doubt he had the funniest motion that had ever been seen in Riverdale. He tied himself in a sort of bowline knot from which his long left arm suddenly protruded, far behind him. Then it came over with a swish like a whiplash, and the ball banged into Krusen's mitt with a report that might well have made a person two streets away wonder where they were blasting.

The big catcher snatched off his glove and stood holding his left hand with an agonized expression, while the crowd roared louder than ever. It was a full minute before the hubbub subsided enough for Krusen to make himself heard. He was scowling with fury at having the laugh turned on himself.

"Don't throw your arm out, you big ape!" he yelled. "Save some of that steam for when you need it." And picking up the ball he slammed it back with venom.

Bill had been standing there, patiently, his grin as broad as ever. He wound up again, without quite so many contortions, and threw another. This time Krusen was prepared, having stuffed a handkerchief under the center of his mitt, and though the ball came in fast he handled it successfully.

"All right," he cried curtly. "Batter up!"

A short, stocky fellow approached the plate, swinging two bats.

"Whoopee!" yelled the crowd. "Got your life insured, Beefy?"

"Huh!" snorted the batter, "that's the kind I like. Put 'em over, Big Boy!" And he stood sturdily up to the rubber, swinging the bat with a short, quick motion.

Bill juggled the ball for a moment, then wound up and pitched.

"Ball *one!*" bellowed a self-appointed umpire in the background.

It was high and far out.

Again the mountain lad unlimbered, and again the voice, "Ball *tuh!*" This one was barely within Krusen's reach, low and outside. A chorus of hoots came from the audience. The batter swung his hickory with a confident leer.

"Here's the platter, Crooked Arm," he cried. "See if you can find it!"

Bill threw another, and it kicked up the dust in front of Beefy's feet. The umpire's "Ball thr-r-ree!" was drowned out by the razzers.

"Oh, oh, oh!" they sang. "Wild as a steer! Crooked Arm! Crooked Arm!"

And Bill went into his knot again, the grin on his face grown a bit uncertain, now. The ball left his hand like a bullet, soaring higher and higher. It passed a good four feet above Krusen's reaching glove, cleared the top of the wire backstop, and smashed through a classroom window.

The catcher tossed his mask into the air. "That's enough for you, Wild Flower!" he chortled. "Back to dear old Hog Back! You'll never make a pitcher in this man's league."

At that moment, as if it had waited for the end of the spectacle, the school gong clanged.

At three-thirty Joe Clark, on his way to the football field for practice, saw Doc Caswell, coach of football and baseball, talking earnestly to Bill Wingate near the entrance to the field. As he approached, Caswell gave Bill's shoulder a pat.

"Try it," he said, and moved on. Joe stopped beside the mountain youth.

"Hello," he said. "Guess the boys got you kind of rattled this noon, didn't they?"

Bill grinned a bit ruefully. "I 'most always git wild when there's a feller battin'," he said. "I'm scairt o' hittin' 'em, I guess. I never like to hurt folks."

Joe grinned sympathetically and passed on. He wondered what the coach had said to Wingate.

. . . .

Bill Wingate made a lot of friends that fall and winter. At first he was ridden pretty hard about his pitching skill, but he took it so good-naturedly that no one kept it up long. No one, that is, except Ed Krusen. The big catcher seemed unable to forget the sting of that first ball and the laughter that had followed it. The only notice he took of the long southpaw was to make an occasional sarcastic remark in his hearing.

The tall youngster was rarely seen about Riverdale after school hours. Each day, promptly at the end of classes, he twirled the crank of his flivver and chugged away up the hills.

"Paw an' I are gettin' out some firewood an' logs for

the sawmill," he explained when Joe Clark asked him why he always went home. Later on, when February gales gave place to March thaws, he explained that sap was running, and he had to go home to tap trees "up in the sugar bush."

It was two or three weeks later that Joe Clark and Red Reynolds felt the restless urge of spring and decided to take a Saturday hike, up on the mountain. They built a fire and ate their lunch in the pine woods somewhere near the north crest of Hog Back, then headed down the ridge.

Half a mile farther on they came to a low, white farmhouse with a barn and outbuildings in the rear. And crossing the yard was a lanky young giant with a brimming sap bucket in each hand. It was Bill Wingate.

"Hi, there!" cried Bill, grinning wider than ever. "How'd you get up in this part o' the country? You're just in time to help taste the first b'ilin'."

They accompanied him out behind the barn where there stood a low board shanty with a stovepipe chimney—the "sugaring-off" shed—and in a few moments the town boys were smacking their lips over the delicious smoky taste of real backwoods maple sugar.

It took them some time to satisfy their exceedingly healthy appetites, but at last they were ready to stop.

Joe sat on a log and looked about at his surroundings curiously.

"Say, Bill," he said, his eyes lifting. "What under the sun is that contraption, over there by the barn."

The mountain boy went suddenly red and began fussing with the stack of tin pails inside the shed. "That?" he said. "Oh, that ain't much of anything."

Joe raised himself and walked over to the barn. For a moment he stood staring, then gave a whistle.

"Hey, Red, come here," he called.

The smaller boy hurried to his side and Bill followed slowly. What they saw was a scarecrow figure of sticks and straw, topped by an old cap. Thrust out at the left, three or four feet from the ground and parallel with the barn wall, was a short length of sapling. And painted on the wall, behind, was a rectangle some fifteen inches wide, extending from eight or ten inches below the top of the dummy figure to a couple of feet above the ground.

Reynolds looked from the strange set-up to his chum and back again without comprehending. But Joe knew what it was.

"Yea, bo!" he cried. "Good for you, Bill! Show us what you do with it."

Bill appeared flustered. "I hadn't figgered anyone would know about this," he said. "I made it to use when there was snow. Doc Caswell told me to do it. It works this way."

He ambled over to the remains of a snowdrift in the lee of the sugar shed and made four or five snowballs. Then he took his position at a distance from the barn and faced them.

"Better not stand too close," he grinned. "You remember that wild pitch last fall? This feller—" he pointed at the scarecrow—"he represents a batter on the opposin' team. I'm in the pitcher's box. Anything I put inside that oblong is a strike—or maybe a home run."

Bill laid down all the snowballs but one, and toed the slab. His wind-up was smoother and quicker than they remembered it, and when he let go of the ball, they heard a crash from the barn like a siege gun. There, in the upper left corner of the rectangle, was a white patch of snow.

Without hurrying, the tall left-hander selected another snowball and threw it. Then another, and another. All of them went over with the same smoking speed. And to the amazement of the watchers, every shot was inside the "strike" area—one close to each corner.

"That last one," said Bill, coming toward the plate, "was just to make sure I could throw one high an' inside without bein' scairt o' the batter."

"Good gravy!" cried Reddy excitedly. "Do you mean to say you *knew* where all those were going?"

"Not just exactly," laughed Bill. "But I've been throwin' so many million snowballs at that barn this winter that I could pretty near hit the place blindfolded. First-off, Paw kicked because it made the stock jump around. But they got used to it. I bet they could go through the battle o' Gettysburg now, an' never wink an eyelash."

Red looked at Joe, then let out a tremendous whoop of joy and rolled on the ground. "Baby!" he yelled, "just wait till old 'Crooked Arm' gets in a game! Wow! I want a reserved seat."

Joe took it more seriously. "The real test is going to be when he faces a flesh-and-blood batter and pitches to a catcher instead of a barn wall," he said thoughtfully.

"Yep," Bill agreed seriously. "Trouble is, I know that dummy there is jest a dummy an' it won't matter if I do hit him."

"Red, it's up to you and me to give Bill a work-out. How about day after tomorrow in the lot back of your house?"

The three held a conference, and a few minutes later the town students were walking down the road, their eyes glowing with anticipation.

.   .   .   .   .   .   °

"First call for baseball candidates!" said a notice on the bulletin board that Tuesday. The previous afternoon Reddy Reynolds, Joe Clark, and Bill Wingate had driven off, immediately after school, in Bill's flivver. Where they had gone they did not say, but the palm of Joe's left hand looked puffy and sore. Reynolds was fairly dancing with excitement as he read the bulletin. He sought out Bill at the lunch hour.

"Today's the day you'll show 'em, Big Boy," he said. "Gee, I can't wait to see Krusen's face. You be there at three-thirty sharp an' get your uniform."

Bill shook his head mournfully. "I got to give up practicin'," he said. "Paw lit into me last night. All the spring plowin's got to be done an' I'll have to beat it straight home after school."

The little redhead's jaw dropped. "Wh—what?" he gasped. "You're not going out for the team this spring? Gosh! The most stuff any pitcher's had for ten years 'round here. And you're goin' to waste it on a plow!"

"You don't understand," Bill put in. "Plowin's somethin' that's *got* to git done, or the family won't eat."

Reddy called Joe over and they did their best to break down the farm boy's argument, but it was no use. Downcast, they watched him drive away when school was over, then turned their steps slowly toward the baseball field.

Riverdale High's prospects looked bright that year. Beefy Talbot, Dolly Madison, and Joe Clark, batting three, four, and five respectively, made up a slugging, fast outfield. Red Reynolds supplied plenty of pepper at shortstop, and Big Ed Krusen, aside from his occasional displays of temperament, was generally conceded to be the best catcher in the Valley Conference. For pitchers they had the veteran Ray Hanson and a flashy newcomer named Billings—a pal of Krusen's. Both were right-handers.

Doc Caswell started the boys off with a rush in their early practice and had them on their toes for the opening game with the University Fresh. Contrary to precedent the college players were weak in pitching, and the Riverdale wrecking crew pounded out such a lead in the first four innings that there was no catching them. The fame of that 6-to-5 victory spread swiftly, and when they followed it up by trimming Connorsville they were hailed by the town as sure winners of the Conference title.

One after another they disposed of the near-by high schools. But down at the other end of the valley was another team with a record almost as imposing. Somerton High's all-veteran aggregation had passed midseason with only one defeat. And they had beaten the

University first-year men by a score of 8-to-o. Somerton was the last game on Riverdale's schedule.

It was the week before that all-important contest, when he was warming up for the Belle Isle game, that Ray Hanson's arm went bad. There was no doubt about it. The bones simply began to creak and the pain in his shoulder made his face go white every time he tried to throw. The coach sent Billings in to pitch.

Belle Isle, not a very formidable foe at best, seemed helpless before Billings' clever shoots. For seven innings none of the invaders got past second base, while the home team bunched half a dozen hits for three runs in the fifth. Then came trouble. Billings acted tired. It was his first attempt of the season to pitch a full game. In the eighth Belle Isle tied the score, and they kept on hitting in the ninth until they had slaughtered Billings' delivery for five more runs.

Faced by that lead, the local players settled down and fought manfully, but the best they could do was squeeze over two more counters.

Beaten by Belle Isle! There was gloom in Riverdale that night, and it still hung over the school on Monday morning when classes began. The single defeat left them tied for honors with Somerton, but their confidence in their ability to win from the down-valley team was sadly shaken. They had just one pitcher—and he wasn't good for a full game.

At noon that Monday, Joe Clark made a bee line for the tree where Bill Wingate's flivver stood. The tall lad from Hog Back was just fishing his lunch out of the rear of the car when Joe seized his arm.

"No time for food now," he said. "Come down to Reddy's house in a hurry!"

"What?" asked Bill, gaping in astonishment. "Can't I even eat?"

"Here," exclaimed the exasperated Joe, "I'm going without *my* lunch for your benefit. Get in and chew fast. I'll drive, myself!"

As they sped down the street he talked.

"See?" he concluded, when they reached the vacant lot. "You don't have to lose a single night's plowing—or hoeing—or whatever it is you're doing now. All you have to do is come over here noons."

Every noon, the next four days, they practiced in Red's back yard, with Clark catching. On Friday, they went with some misgivings to Doc Caswell and gave the surprised coach a demonstration on the deserted diamond. Doc's eyes opened wide at Bill's uncanny control, and he grinned with satisfaction at Bill's fast ball.

"Go to the plate, Red," he ordered Reynolds. "Swing at 'em."

Inwardly Red groaned. All their secret practices hadn't removed Bill's fear of hitting the batter. But Bill's first two pitches to Red were just where Clark called for them. Dazzlingly they cut the outside corner. Then, hopefully, the catcher called for an inside ball, and from that moment, Bill began to get wild. Hope faded from the coach's eyes.

"He gets that way," Joe Clark said helplessly, after Bill had heaved one over his head, "when he pitches to a live batter. I thought he had it licked. He practiced against his barn, the way you told him, with a dummy batter, all winter. And Red and I've been working him out—"

Bill Wingate walked up from the mound with a regretful grin on his freckled face. "Guess I'm no good," he said. "I'm sorry."

The coach looked at the tall student keenly. "There's no chance in the world of your hitting a batter," he said sharply. "With that control you'll never hit one."

"But if I did—"

"You can't!" Doc interrupted.

"I jes' see that batter standin' there—"

"That's the trouble! You see him. You're not looking at the catcher; you're looking at the batter!"

For several minutes the coach talked earnestly to Bill Wingate, and ended by ordering him to be in uniform the next day. But when he left the three boys, imperceptibly he shook his head.

.   .   .   .

The game was scheduled for two-thirty, but even before noon the cars and buses had begun to stream up the valley road. Riverdale boasted a stand that seated nearly three thousand, and it was filled to overflowing by two o'clock. Hundreds of other spectators stood coatless in the hot June sun, watching the two nines practice.

The Somerton boys were in high fettle, whooping it up and snapping the ball back and forth across the infield with big league deftness. There was little noise among the home team. Gathered around Doc Caswell on the third base bench they listened grim-faced to his instructions, and when the time came they trotted out to their places, quietly. Krusen, crouched behind the plate, contributed the only noise. He was "talking it up," trying to steady Billings, who looked nervous and self-conscious out there on the hill.

The Somerton lead-off man waited him out and earned a base on balls, but after that the pitcher settled down. He had a nice hopping fast ball and a fair drop, and with Krusen's signals he was mixing them nicely. The side was retired without a run.

Somerton started a chunky southpaw with a deceptive delivery, and the game settled down into a pitchers' battle. Up to the beginning of the sixth the scoreboard showed only zeros for both teams. In the first half of that inning the visitors began to hit. The first man up singled, but was out trying to steal. Then came a two-base hit, an infield single, and a walk, in swift succession. The stands groaned, but the groan became a triumphant yell when little Red Reynolds snapped up a wicked grounder, touched second, and doubled the runner at first with a magnificent throw.

Riverdale went to bat eager for gore. Beefy Talbot marched up to the plate and hit the first ball pitched for a sizzling two-bagger. Dolly Madison waited for a good one, and when it came he pounded out a long single, scoring his teammate.

Before the cheering had time to die down, Joe Clark, last of the slugging trio, took a toehold and smashed the ball out of the lot. The rally ended there, but the home fans looked fondly at the figure "3" in the run column.

Then history began to repeat. Somerton kept up its hitting in the seventh and Billings weakened visibly, just as he had done in the Belle Isle game. He passed two men. The third one up flied out to Talbot, but the fourth singled to deep short.

With three on bases the next batter hit a short, bobbling grounder straight at the pitcher. He muffed it, then picked it up and threw wild in an effort to catch the man running home. The ball rolled to the backstop before Krusen could stop it, and one run crossed the rubber.

Riverdale breathed more easily when the rival pitcher stepped up and struck out. But there were still three Somerton boys dancing on the bags and the top of the batting order was coming up. The lead-off man waited till he had three balls and a strike and then picked out a grooved ball and walloped it savagely for a double. Two runners loped across the plate and the third, racing the throw-in, slid safely across, to the tune of Somerton's frenzied howling.

"Take him out! Take him out!" Riverdale town fans yelled, unaware that Billings' only relief was an awkward boy from Hog Back.

Billings, obviously unnerved, had a conference with the catcher, then shuffled back to his box. He threw three straight balls, and the yells increased. The fourth pitch was hit almost on a line to right field. Joe Clark jumped far into the air, caught it in his bare hand, and brought the nightmare inning to a close.

The Riverdale players came to bat, fighting discouragement. Billings was blowing up. One after another, three batters went up to the plate and flied out—struck out—grounded out. The score was 4 to 3 and it was the beginning of the eighth.

There was some commotion around the home-town players' bench as they prepared to take the field. The coach had been talking to Joe Clark and Reddy Reynolds. Now he stood up and issued an order. There was a moment of dumbfounded silence; then the hubbub started. Big Ed Krusen slammed his mask and mitt on the ground and pulled angrily to loosen the strap of his chest pad.

"What!" he yelled. "That guy—that Crooked Arm? Why, he's wild as a hawk! I'll be darned if I'll catch him!"

The coach eyed him coldly. "All right," he said, "there's the bench. Here, Clark, put 'em on. You'll catch. And you, Mack——" he summoned a substitute—"you'll take right field. And Wingate—remember what I told you!"

The crowd looked at the pitcher's box expectantly. There was no sign of Billings. Instead there ambled out to the hill a huge, lanky youngster in a pair of old blue baseball pants and a sweat shirt, both much too small for him. His sandy hair was bare to the sun and he was grinning.

Hoots of laughter went up all around the field.

"Where'd you get this one, Riverdale?" a Somerton

rooter bellowed. "Put him back in the bean patch!" And a steady fire of jeers greeted the boy as he took his stand and began to throw practice balls.

"Look at that motion! Whoopee!" squealed the on-lookers. Some of them quieted down when they saw the sphere come smoking into Clark's mitt, but there was still plenty of noise when the batter stepped into position.

He was a cocky youngster—number three in the visitors' batting order.

"Come on, you Lefty!" he cried raucously. "Bet a nickel you can't put one over the pan."

Before he could draw back his bat the long southpaw burned a strike past him. At that the yells began to come from the other side.

"Let's see you do that again!" yelled the batter with injured pride, and he waggled his stick viciously.

Clark laid one finger in the mitt and Bill nodded. Whish! The ball was high inside and the batter dodged.

"Str-r-ike!" called the umpire.

The loud protests of the Somerton bench were unavailing. Three fingers in the catcher's glove—the signal for a low ball. Bill wound up deliberately and brought his arm over fast. Bang! The ball had cut the corner and turned Joe Clark three-quarters of the way around, while the batsman was still getting his swing under way.

The umpire's "You're out!" was drowned by a roar from the Riverdale stands, as another victim walked up to the plate. Clark showed four fingers, and Bill, getting the signal, tossed a wide one—a teaser—that made the batter settle back to wait. It was a fatal error. Two clean strikes flashed past him, and swinging desperately at the next one he knocked a sky-high foul that came down into Joe's big glove!

Two out, now, and Bill proceeded to bear down. The oldest fan in Riverdale couldn't remember such speed as he put on the next two balls he pitched. He literally threw them past the batter, after the manner of Lefty Grove. The Somerton man was a slugger with a reputation for hitting fast ones. He gripped his bat and drew it back, grimly determined.

Bill wound up elaborately while the crowd grew quiet. Over came that long left arm and the batter swung with all his might. Slowly as a summer breeze the ball drifted by and the Somerton player spun twice around with the effort of his blow.

A mighty roar rose from the bleachers and the Riverdale men looked like a different team as they raced in from the field. Beefy Talbot seized three bats and swung them vigorously as he approached the plate. The stands were still roaring as the stocky outfielder took his first strike. Calmly he took a ball, another ball, and then laced a beauty down the third-base line for a single.

Dolly Madison swung mightily at the first pitch and hit a long fly to center. There was a breathless instant of suspense, then a groan, as the ball showed safe in the fielder's glove.

Joe Clark up. He took his time, giving Talbot a chance to rattle the pitcher by a series of false steals. Then one came over that suited him, and he smote it viciously. The ball crossed the infield on a screaming line, bounced high as the right fielder ran in for it, and rolled past him toward the open spaces. Talbot was away like a flash. He rounded third as the fielder recovered the ball and sprinted home just ahead of the throw.

When the dust cleared away the score was tied—and Clark was standing on third.

Up to the plate stepped little Reddy Reynolds, bristling like a bantam rooster.

"Out of the lot, kid! Make it a homer!" yelled the excited crowd, and Red held his bat as if that were exactly what he meant to do. But as the pitcher started the throw, the carrot-top suddenly shifted his grip. He met the ball with a beautiful bunt that rolled tantalizingly toward third and Joe's flying cleats dented the plate.

While the Riverdale populace howled its approval,

Reynolds took a long lead off first and prepared to go down on the next pitch. But Mack, the substitute outfielder, whose turn had come at bat, tapped a hard roller straight to second and Red, racing down the base path, found the ball there ahead of him. An easy toss to first doubled the hitter and the eighth inning was over.

Five to four at the beginning of the ninth, with Riverdale on top once more! There was a ceaseless, hoarse roar from the stands. Bill Wingate strolled out to the box, serene amid the noise. There was no haste in his motions and no delay. But his speed was blinding. The first ball pitched was a called strike, the second a foul. On the third the batter swung and missed. The bass drummer in the Riverdale band banged his drum, and Bill grinned and watched the next man come up.

In response to Joe's signal, the big left-hander threw a low one over the outside corner—his fourth strike in four pitched balls.

"Hey!" yelled the batter, turning around. "Put a new ball in. I couldn't see it because it was dirty!"

The umpire produced a snow-white ball and Bill wound up again. The Somerton man made a futile cut at it as it flashed by.

"What was the reason that time?" somebody asked, and a bellow of laughter followed.

HE WHIPPED IT TOWARD THE WAITING FIRST-
SACKER

As the ball came back to the mound, the southpaw caught it and threw it without a wind-up—a sizzling third strike that caught the batter flat-footed.

Again the big drum pounded and the crowd cheered, but Bill paid no attention to them. He was running toward the plate, where Joe Clark stood, looking at the bruised, purple palm of his catching hand.

"Think you can last out the inning?" asked Bill in an undertone.

"Sure," Joe answered. "Burn 'em in, Bill. Gosh, how those fast ones make 'em swing!"

And Bill went back to the box. Obedient to Joe's signal he put all he had on the first ball. It was over the center—and the batter was late. The seventh straight strike!

Clark laid two fingers in the mitt and called for another fast one, but Bill shook his head. He had seen Joe's arm wince and his face whiten when he handled that pitch. Slowly the mountain boy wound up and threw a soft one, right over the plate. The bat connected with a solid smash and a screeching liner came past Bill. He stuck out his hand and knocked the ball down. There it went, rolling slowly toward first, and the batter was halfway to the bag. He rushed out and grabbed up the ball. With all the power in his long arm he whipped it toward the waiting first-sacker, and the Somerton man was out by inches.

.   .   .   .

When it came to carrying heroes off the field, Riverdale was not to be outdone by anybody. In a roaring mob, the supporters of the home team surged across the diamond and lifted three players to their shoulders. They were Red Reynolds, Joe Clark, and the lanky farmer boy from Hog Back. Doc Caswell, pushing through the crowd, reached up a hand to the long southpaw.

"Good pitching, Big Boy," he said.

Bill grinned back at him. "I took your medicine, Coach," he chuckled. "I never thought about the batter at all—jest pretended I was throwin' snowballs at a barn!"

THE CARRABESCOOK
DOUBLES

"SURE, it's a hard name to say," wrote Bill Evans to his friend Walt Greenway. "Most of these old Maine Indian names are. It's pronounced Car-ra-bes-cook, with the accent on the BES. But as a matter of fact you won't have to pronounce it at all. You just bail out of the train at North Carry and I'll be waiting for you with the bus. Don't forget to bring that trusty paddle of yours."

It was Walt's first visit to Maine. With his suitcase, duffle-bag, and big spruce paddle in the seat beside him, he looked out of the window of the grimy little local that was taking him north from Portland.

They puffed away up a green valley and gradually the hills began to rise into deep, cool-looking pine woods, and stony farms with cattle grazing in the fields. There were few vacationists on the train. Most of the passengers were country people, chatting in a down-East twang that delighted Walt's ears.

By noon the farms had become fewer, the hills higher and more rugged. Blue lakes gleamed through gaps in the ranges. The train clanked up to a weather-beaten little box of a station and the brakeman called, "Nawth Carry—Nawth Carry!"

As Walt bundled his luggage off on the platform he looked eagerly for Bill. But there was no sign of him or his car. The station lay in a flat clearing, under the glare of the noonday sun. There was only one living thing in sight—a lanky figure in flannel shirt and high-laced boots, squatting with his back against the station. His old felt hat was over his eyes and apparently he was asleep.

Walt tried the station door and found it locked. Nothing to do but wait. He sat on his suitcase and whistled mournfully. This seemed to rouse his solitary neighbor, who pushed back his hat, squinted at him through drowsy eyes, and finally rose with a grunt.

"Hi," said the man. "Ain't lookin' fer a guide, be you?"

He was bigger than he had looked sitting down—well over six feet tall and heavy-shouldered. There was every reason why Walt should have been thrilled at his first meeting with a real Maine guide, but something about the man's hard eyes gave him a feeling of dislike.

"No," he explained briefly. "I'm waiting for a friend to meet me."

"Where 'bouts are you headin'?" asked the guide, eying the luggage.

"Carrabescook Lake," Walt replied. "Evans' camp on Horseshoe Cove."

"Yeah, I know who ye mean," nodded the man. "Tow-headed boy, 'bout eighteen? Drives an old rattle-trap? Well, if he can't find ye some good bass, send fer me. I know every ledge an' hole in the lake. Buck Peavy's my name. My shack's over on the south shore."

He went slouching off across the clearing, and a few minutes later Walt heard a rattling sound from up the road.

"Yippee!" howled Bill Evans, as his car burst out of the woods. "Sorry I'm late. The old lady popped a tire back a way."

The two boys presented a striking contrast as they shook hands: Bill, with sun-bleached hair and skin brown as an Indian's, wearing a sleeveless jersey and an old pair of sailor pants; Walt, dark-haired and pale of face, dressed in neat city clothes.

"Come on, you old tenderfoot," laughed Bill. "Let's get up to camp and find you some sunburn."

They bundled Walt's belongings into the rear seat and chugged off, up the road.

Carrabescook Lake, Bill explained, was seven miles long, and Horseshoe Cove lay three miles up the shore.

Walt could see blue stretches of incredible beauty between the pines that shaded the road. Across the lake, heavily forested mountain ridges went up steeply from the water. It was the kind of place he had dreamed about, all his life.

They parked the car behind the comfortable cottage and went in to greet Dr. and Mrs. Evans. Ten minutes later Walt was in his bathing suit, touring the surroundings. The camp was perched on a ledge of granite that rose sheer out of the lake.

"How's that for a dive?" grinned Bill. "It goes straight off, thirty feet deep!"

Below, near the foot of the ledge, was the boathouse and a stout wooden dock with a springboard at its outer end. They had a swim in the cold Maine water and then went to lunch.

Afterward Bill led the way to the boathouse.

"The bass ought to be biting, over by Deer Island," he said. "Pick yourself a rod. Shall we paddle or use the outboard?"

"You know me," Walt replied. "I'd rather paddle a canoe than eat."

The canoe was a green-painted sixteen-footer, light and slim.

"Father got her years ago, for one-man carries," Bill remarked. "She's not as seaworthy as some—too slender in the beam. But boy, is she fast! We call her the Green Arrow."

He patted the craft's bottom, pointing to various patches. "That one we got on the Allegash trip, two summers back," he said. "This long one is a souvenir of White Rip, down the gorge, below the outlet dam. Thought I was a goner that time. We wound up in the pool at the foot of the rapids half full of water, but she didn't upset."

"Gee!" murmured Walt. "Let's go down there some day. I've never shot any rapids, you know."

Bill hesitated. "It's pretty stiff water," he said. "But a chap that's as much at home in a canoe as you ought to be able to do it. Sure—I'll go down with you. Better get used to the boat first, though."

Walt, who was four or five pounds lighter than his host, took the bow seat.

"Gosh!" said Bill, "it's good to have a real paddler in front. Look how she slides along!"

A westerly breeze sent small blue waves chuckling along the side. The boys swung their blades in a steady rhythm of contentment.

"I'll say she's fast," Walt laughed. "We must be doing six an hour right now."

"Easy," Bill agreed. "There isn't a boat on the lake

that can touch her. With the right crew she could win the Carrabescook Doubles."

"What's that?" Walt asked.

"Well, it's about the biggest canoe race in this part of Maine. It's held a week from next Saturday, and all the best paddlers from miles around will be in it. Dad and I tried last year but we came in last. He's strong enough, but he gets winded in about two minutes and this race is half a mile. It's fun to watch, though. I'm glad you'll be here to see it."

Walt took several strokes before he replied. Then: "What do you mean—see it?" he asked. "Maybe you and I could show 'em something. I ought to be in top shape by then."

Bill laughed. "You don't understand," he said. "We'd be up against half a dozen crews of guides—huskies who paddle from twenty to fifty miles a day, six months of the year. They come up from Rangeley and down from Moosehead, and they sure can put wings on a canoe. Still," he mused, "if you don't mind taking a licking, it might be fun to go in."

The canoe slipped into the shadow of the hemlocks that fringed Deer Island. "All right," said Bill, "get out your rod. I'll paddle slow. Anywhere along this ledge is good bass ground."

Walt reached back for the bait box. "What'll I try 'em with first?" he asked. "A grasshopper?"

He picked out a big green fellow and flicked him along the surface in short jumps, then let him come to a momentary rest. There was a flash of spray as a fish broke water—and the rod tingled to a clean strike.

"Good!" said Bill. "Give him line—little more—there, it's slack. Reel in fast!"

For three or four hectic minutes Walt played his fish, then got him alongside, within reach of the net. It was a shining black bass, nearly twenty inches long.

Bill stared. "Say—talk about beginner's luck!" he exclaimed. "That baby'll weigh four pounds or better. I've caught only one as big as that all summer."

They were still admiring the fish when another canoe slipped silently from behind a point of rocks. The boys looked up at the sound of a drawling voice and saw a big man slouched in the stern, his rod lying across the thwart in front of him.

"Any luck?" he asked, laconically.

"You're dog-gone right!" returned Bill. "My pal hooked this fellow half a minute after he baited up!"

Walt was watching the lanky paddler closely, for he was certain it was the guide who had introduced himself that morning. But the man gave no sign of recognition. His mouth twisted into a sardonic grin, and he shifted his quid of tobacco to spit expertly over the side.

"Nice-lookin' fish," he nodded. "Reckon he's the one I jest threw back."

"Huh!" Bill snorted. "Too bad if you did, because you'll never catch him again. Walt's going to have him for supper."

The man's long arms straightened with an effortless sweep of the paddle that shot his shabby canoe a dozen yards down shore. "Oh, well," his drawl came back to them—"I know where ther's plenty bigger."

Bill chuckled. "You just met a character," said he. "That's Joe Peavy, one of the smartest guides and biggest liars in Maine."

"Yes, I saw him at North Carry," Walt replied. "Only I thought he told me his name was Buck."

"That's Joe's twin brother," Bill explained. "They look alike and talk alike, but Joe's harmless and Buck's not. He runs booze for the lumber camps in the winter. Boy, you ought to see those twins drive a canoe, though! They won the Doubles two years ago—lost, last summer, to a pair from up North."

They fished for another hour and landed four more bass. As they swung the canoe homeward, Walt sighed happily. "I don't know whether it's the air up here, or what," he said, "but I feel great—ready for anything."

He hesitated a moment. "I had a reason for thinking we might do something in that race," he said. "They held the National Canoe Regatta on the Schuylkill this summer, and I watched them pretty carefully. Tell me— how do these guide crews sit in the boat?"

"They don't sit," answered Bill. "They kneel on the bottom."

"Bow and stern?" Walt pursued.

"Sure. Where else would they be?"

Walt grinned. "I'd have asked the same question myself, a month ago," he said. "But the doubles stars from the big canoe clubs both kneel amidships!"

"Sounds foolish," Bill put in. "Who does the steering?"

"Nobody has to steer," Walt explained. "That's the beauty of it. Steering wastes effort. With two paddlers in the middle neither one pulls the other around. The pair of Washington boys who won the national junior doubles weren't a bit bigger than you, and didn't look as strong. But did they fly!"

"Well, you've got to show me," said Bill. "We'll try it after supper."

That evening, in the gathering dusk, the boys went down to the dock again. Walt directed Bill to kneel on his right knee, just forward of the middle of the canoe, ready to paddle on the right. He took his own station a yard aft, crouched on his left knee, and pushed off.

"Now," he said, "set yourself for a good, fast stroke. I'll come in with you on the beat. The way we're placed we won't interfere with each other."

Bill plunged his paddle. "Stroke," he called "—stroke —stroke—" and Walt timed his swing to match. The canoe shot ahead like a green streak.

"Gosh!" gasped Bill.

"Now we'll turn," Walt panted, and dug in his paddle in reverse. The light craft spun about almost in its own length, and five seconds later they were tearing for home once more.

Bill's face shone with more than perspiration as they drifted up to the dock. "That's faster than I ever hoped to travel in a canoe!" he said soberly. "Boy, we've got something!"

For a week the weather held fair. Walt, out all day long in the sun, put on a tan that made Bill's look pale, and gained four pounds in twice as many days. And every evening as soon as it grew dusk, they held secret race practice in the canoe.

Bill, with the aid of a steel tape, had laid out a course close to the shore that duplicated as nearly as possible the route of the big doubles race. It was a quarter-mile straightaway, with a single turn around a buoy at the upper end. They went over it once or twice each night, learning how fast a stroke they could hit and hold—practicing the turn till they could spin the craft on a dime.

It was on Thursday evening—two days before the race—that Joe Peavy paid a call at the Evans camp. He came shambling in, big-shouldered and bashful, twiddling his old felt hat in his hands.

"Buck and me was wonderin'," he began, when fish, the weather, and other topics had been exhausted, "if you'd let us hire your canoe fer the race, Sat'day. I reckon it's 'bout the fastest boat in these parts."

He had addressed himself to Dr. Evans, but Bill broke in with a laugh. "Not this year, Joe," he said. "Guess you haven't heard that we're going to win that race—Walt and I."

Peavy's poker face showed no surprise. " 'Course," he replied, "if you're usin' it, there's no more to be said. Goin' to win, eh? Well, that's interestin'."

He grinned and shuffled out. That night the rain drummed on the roof above the boys' bunks, and morning dawned gray and cloudy.

"The bass won't be biting today," said Bill at breakfast, "but we might try that trip down the gorge. Plenty of water after the rain."

Walt agreed with enthusiasm and they made an early

start. At a point near the outlet dam they took the canoe out of the water. Bill pointed to a rough board shack, half concealed by the trees. "That's the Peavy boys' place," he said. "Don't see anybody around, though."

They shouldered the canoe and struck into a curving carry-path through the woods. A hundred yards down the trail, Walt, in the rear, thought he heard a stick snap behind him. He turned his head as far as the canoe would allow, but there was nothing in sight.

"What do you suppose that noise was?" he whispered.

Bill strode steadily forward. "Getting nervous?" he laughed. "I didn't hear anything. Might have been a dog or a porcupine."

In a moment they came out on the bank of a narrow, swift-flowing river.

"The white water starts a quarter of a mile below," said Bill. "Gives us time to get set before we hit it. Only takes about a minute to go through, but it'll seem longer than that. I'll steer. You just balance, and fend off the rocks if we get too close."

They shoved off, gliding swiftly down with the current. Walt, kneeling tensely in the bow, searched the water ahead for the first sign of the rapids. As they rounded a bend there was a gleam of white ahead, and suddenly they were in it. The canoe shot down a smooth glissade of water and leaped like a bucking horse on the wave at its foot. Bill swung the nose of the craft dexterously from side to side, avoiding the masses of wet rock that thrust their ugly heads out of the spray.

Walt crouched with paddle poised, thrilling to the rush of their descent. Once, at a sharp cry from the steersman, he took a quick, desperate stroke on the left, and they skirted the black snout of a ledge that had been hidden by a wave crest. Then, as suddenly as it had come, the surging rapid lay behind them, and they floated in an eddy, close to a pebbly shore.

"Here we are," laughed Bill, "safe and sound. There's a spring back here in the woods a way. Let's get a drink before we carry back."

They hauled the canoe out on shore and entered the spruce bush. It took them perhaps twenty minutes to reach the spring and return.

As Bill started to pick up his end of the canoe, he stooped suddenly and stared at the bottom. There was a gaping hole through the canvas, and the ribs and planking were splintered upward, inside.

"Gosh all fishhooks!" cried Walt in dismay. "Did you feel it when we hit? I thought we came through without a scratch!"

Bill's brow gathered darkly. "We did," he answered. "This was done since we left."

He turned and looked carefully about. The shelving beach was made up of pebbles and small stones. But in the yellow foam at the edge of the pool he found a larger rock, big as a man's head.

"Look," said Bill. "That stone's half out of water, and yet it's wet all over." He picked it up and looked closely at each rough point and projection.

"Here's what I was hunting for," he exclaimed at last, and Walt saw a speck of green paint clinging to a sharp edge.

"Well," Bill went on, regretfully, "there goes the race, I guess." He dropped the stone and laid hold of the canoe. They were climbing the carry-path along the bank when Walt called sharply, "Wait!"

There was a faint track in the wet earth—the print of a big, nail-studded boot. "Somebody was here this morning," said Walt, "since the rain."

"Somebody with a grudge against us," Bill nodded. "I should have paid more attention when you heard that noise. He was following us."

When they arrived, puffing, at the dam, Bill stuffed a double handful of grass into the hole in the canoe bottom. They returned slowly to camp, Walt bailing constantly with a bait can while Bill paddled. It was a gloomy pair of boys who greeted Dr. Evans at the dock. They pulled the light craft out on the planks and Bill pointed to the hole. "What do you think, Dad?" he asked. "Can it be patched?"

His father whistled. "I never tried one as bad as that," he said, "but we'll see what we can do as soon as she's dry."

By noon the sun had come out and the moisture evaporated quickly. As soon as lunch was over they went down to the dock, armed with materials for patching.

Luckily, no piece of planking had broken completely away. Under pressure, the tough cedar wood bent back into place and was secured there by a light cleat, screwed to the solid ribs on either side. Next they filled the outside of the break with plastic wood, smoothing it to the contour of the hull. When it had hardened they carefully cut away the ragged edges of the tear and smeared the under side of the canvas around the hole with canoe glue.

Bill cut an oval of fine-woven patching canvas. To it he applied the glue with as much care as if he had been painting a miniature, and set the oval in place with deft fingers. Then he pressed down the surrounding edges in a clean, overlapping welt, and for ten minutes he rubbed the surface of the patch till it lay tight and smooth.

"Nothing to do now but wait and hope," said Dr.

Evans. "We'll let it dry overnight and paint it in the morning."

. . . .

Saturday! Walt woke with a beam of golden sunlight in his eyes and excitement tingling in his veins. Then like a dash of cold water came remembrance of yesterday's catastrophe. Would the patch hold? And if it did, would the speed of the canoe be cut down?

Long before breakfast the boys were down at the boathouse. To all appearances the work of the day before was solid and strong. Bill got a can of green paint—quick-drying enamel—and laid a smooth coat over and around the patch. By eleven o'clock it was thoroughly dry.

"She could stand a second coat," said Bill frowning, "but it would still be wet. We'll chance her as she is."

They slipped the canoe into the lake, paddled slowly a mile up shore and returned. From his place in the stern, Walt watched the repaired spot anxiously, but not a drop of water entered.

"Hot darn!" cried Bill, in his relief. "She's as good as ever! And will the polecat that did it get a jolt when he sees us this afternoon!"

"You think he'll be there?" asked Walt.

"I think," said Bill, slowly, "that he'll not only be there—he'll be paddling against us in the race."

Dr. Evans' advice to go light on the lunch was unnecessary. At the moment they were too high-strung to be tempted by food. By one-thirty they were ready to start their two-mile paddle to the Carrabescook Club. Bill slipped a spare paddle into the bottom of the canoe, for use in case of accidents. He was using a favorite of his own, and Walt had the big spruce blade he had brought from Philadelphia.

They took their time and it was after two when they joined the fleet of canoes and motor boats converging toward the clubhouse dock. The judges were already registering the entries for the race. Around the table where they gave their names, a dozen guides were joking and laying bets. Most of them were strangers from up- and down-state—big, bronzed men in woods garb, some barefooted, some wearing moccasins or sneakers. Bill pointed out such notables as he knew.

"There's Injun Charlie and Big Joe Beaulieu, from Moosehead," he whispered. "Won last year. They've got a real birch-bark canoe that's plenty fast."

Among the last to enter were a pair of husky young men in blue Yale crew jerseys—counselors from the boys' camp at the head of the lake.

"Where are the Peavys?" asked Walt. "I haven't seen them around."

"They're here," Bill replied. "Already in their boat. I spotted them when we landed."

One of the judges rose and lifted a megaphone. "Time to call the race!" he shouted. He read the list of entries over, eleven canoes in all. Their positions had been drawn by lot, but as Bill explained, position in this race meant little. The boys' boat had fifth place. The rules were announced. One quarter mile to the buoy, which must be rounded with a left turn; one quarter mile back to the finish—a straight line between the end of the dock and the judges' boat. Any canoe fouling or interfering with another to be disqualified from the race.

One by one, the crews got into their canoes. Bill and Walt were among the last. On the way down to the shore, Walt seized his friend's arm and pointed. Lying at the foot of a big pine were a pair of hob-nailed high boots.

"Say!" muttered Bill, stooping quickly. "What did I tell you? The fellow's here. One of these boots made the track we saw!"

All the other canoes were on the lake when they pushed off. There was a light, steady breeze from the west, but the waves were not troublesome. The boys knelt in the bottom amidships and took up their paddles. For a moment their unusual position went unnoticed. Then one of the guides caught sight of them.

"Hey, kids," he shouted impatiently, "you're holdin' up the race. Say—what in Sam Hill—look at 'em, Elmer! What kind o' paddlin' do ye call that?"

There was a chorus of laughter and gibes from the starting line, as the boys moved into place, but they were too intent on the job in hand to be perturbed. Walt stole a glance along the line. All the others—even the two Yale men—were kneeling in orthodox fashion, at bow and stern.

"How do you feel?" he asked Bill.

"Swell!" the other replied. "Only I wish they'd start us."

There was a short interval of jockeying to get the canoes evenly lined up. Then from the judges' boat came a megaphoned call—"Fifteen seconds to go . . . ten seconds . . . five seconds" . . . and at last the crashing report of a gun.

Twenty-two paddles flashed into action with the sound. "Stroke!" barked Bill—"Stroke!—Stroke!" Then his voice was drowned in the yells of paddlers and spectators. The boys had practiced together so long that they worked in perfect unison. But the tense excitement of the start had sent them away at a feverish beat. At the end of a hundred yards they were bunched with three other canoes in the lead.

Walt felt strong and eager, but he knew the stroke

was too fast. "Slower!" he urged. "Long and steady— attaboy!"

They dug deep and drove their paddles far back; swinging in rhythm to take advantage of the "run." A dingy black canoe had crept ahead, its broad-backed crew paddling like mad. Walt, snatching a glimpse to make sure he was on the course, recognized the Peavy twins as the leading pair. As the race neared the quarter-mile buoy they were a full boat length in front, and steadily widening the open water between their canoe and the boys'.

Two other crews were almost abreast of the Green Arrow, both of them off to the right. But now another craft appeared at Walt's shoulder, coming up on the left in a desperate effort to get inside the boys on the turn. A birch-bark bow—Injun Charlie.

"Come on!" yelled Walt. "Faster!"

They drove their paddles furiously and pulled away, inch by inch. Walt held the canoe's nose a yard to the right of the bobbing black-and-white barrel that marked the turn. The Peavys had already passed it and were coming about with a mighty splash of paddles.

"Now!" shouted Bill. Walt braced his broad blade, holding the light craft like a pivot. And in three lightning strokes they were around. That spinning turn changed the whole race in an instant. Instead of trail-

THE FINAL FURLONG WAS A NIGHTMARE

ing, the boys were leading by a length as they started the grueling drive for the finish.

"Steady!" panted Walt, grimly. He knew they would be challenged, and soon. They were halfway down the stretch, and the howl of the crowd was audible through the drumming in his ears. His back and arms were racked by a mighty weariness. Over his shoulder he caught a glimpse of two canoes almost abreast—the black Peavy boat, and the flash of blue Yale jerseys. And just at that instant he realized that his knee was wet. There was water welling through the patch in the canoe bottom!

"Let's go!" gasped Bill. "We can do it!" And he raised the stroke—faster—faster.

That final furlong was a nightmare. Walt's arms felt like chunks of wood, and his breath came in sobs through his teeth. But they held the terrific stroke and fairly lifted the sinking boat through the water.

Bow to bow the three canoes swept down to the finish. There was a snapping of wood and a splash. The Yale men had broken a paddle—capsized.

Only seconds to go now and they were holding even. Then, with a vicious twist of his paddle, Buck Peavy swung the prow of the black boat almost into them. Bill's blade never faltered. It drove down cleanly into the narrow gap between the two canoes, and without swerving, the Green Arrow shot over the line.

Walt felt himself reeling forward and everything went black. When he opened his eyes again he was lying on a carpet of pine needles with Bill bending over him.

"Are you all right?" his chum panted anxiously.

"Sure," croaked Walt, with a grin. "Who won?"

"We did—by a gnat's eyelash!" said Bill. "And that squares accounts with the Peavys. The last thing I saw before they slunk off was Buck pulling on those hob-nailed boots."

QUICK KICK

THAT'S the new play. Like every good play in football, it takes eleven men—each doing his job."

Coach "Hike" Kilroy's steely eyes flashed around the darkening room. He picked up an eraser and swept it through the circles, crosses, and running lines of the blackboard diagram. Then he swung back to his audience.

"I've one more thing to say. Some of you hope for a Conference championship. But if you keep on letting them block your punts you're going to get licked." For a few seconds he let the words sink in. "All right," he said shortly. "That's all for tonight."

The Varsity squad rose and filed from the room in silence. Outside, their voices rose in laughter and fragments of song, but Barry Hughes, 200-pound tackle and captain, stayed behind, his face serious.

"Walking over, Coach?" he asked.

Kilroy nodded and they went slowly down the path. A fading October sunset shed golden light across the Cameron campus. There was a nip in the air—good football weather.

"This blocked punt business," Hughes began, "I think we can stop it, Coach. It's the left side of the line they break through. Hartley and Wiggins are strong enough but they need experience. Couldn't we work on that this week, and tighten up those holes?"

"We're going to," the coach replied. "But you know where the real trouble lies. It's Butch Davis. A grand punter, but slow. He has to take three steps to get the ball away, and I can't break him of it."

He paused a moment, and when he went on there was an edge of bitterness in his voice. "We've got the fastest pair of ends in the Conference," he said. "I'd hoped to shoot in a quick kick play this year. It's one of the smartest tricks in the bag when it's done right. Boy, how we could use Jack Moran and Weasel Blake down the field, if we had a real quick-kicker! But I've combed the squad and there isn't a man in the lot that can boot one fast enough."

They said good night at a fork in the path, and Barry Hughes departed in the direction of the Commons. Kilroy's way led past the practice field toward his house on Faculty Circle. There was a thud of leather, over on his left. Four or five students were kicking up and down the field in the dusk. It was too dark to see much, but the coach stopped a moment to watch them, his mind still busy with team problems.

Suddenly he was all attention. The boys were playing one of those kicking games where, if you catch the ball, you can punt it at once, and if you miss you take three steps backward from the point where it is touched. A long, high spiral came down the field, and a boy ran sidewise to get under it. He caught the ball in his hands, took one brief step, and sent it whirling back with a low, hard-driven punt that angled to the right. There was frantic scurrying at the other end of the field. The ball took a high bounce, cleared the head of the nearest man, and rolled to within a yard of the goal line.

The boy who had kicked it laughed aloud. "Take yo' three steps in reverse," he shouted, "an' let's see what y'all can do!"

The receiver made a desperate effort. From deep in the end zone the pigskin sailed up and up, till Kilroy lost it in the darkness. Not so the boy he had been watching. Sprinting forward from midfield, he was well inside the 30-yard line when the soaring punt came down in his arms.

Again he wasted no time. "Look out—it's a drop-kick!" cried one of his opponents, rushing to get behind the goal posts. But the ball beat him. From the ground in front of the kicker's toe it described a neat arc over the center of the bar, and bounced uncaught on the other side.

"Hi-yah! Another two bits!" crowed the winner, doing a war dance. "Yo' cain't deny that one!"

He was starting at a trot for the side line when Kilroy's gruff voice halted him.

"Hold on, son," he said. "Are you a student here?"

"Yes, suh."

"Freshman?"

"No, suh—sophomore."

"What's your name?"

"Warfill Jones. But they call me 'Waffle,' mostly."

"Ever play football?"

"In our little ol' high school, back home. Yes, suh."

"Where's that?"

"Warfill Co't House—in the Valley o' Virginia, suh!" He said those last words with a pride and reverence that conjured up pictures. Barefoot marchers in tattered gray, and Marse Robert himself, on Traveler.

"Not very big, are you?" said the coach. "What do you weigh?"

"Hundred an' fifty-five, right about."

"You're not out for football here. Why not? Don't you like the game?"

"Sho' I like it. Trouble is, I jerk sodas fo' my keep, an' the busiest time o' day is from three o'clock till five-thirty. Only time I git fo' playin' is when other folks go home to supper."

Kilroy stroked his chin and thought. "How much do you make, at the soda fountain?" he asked.

"Six dollars a week an' bo'd. But I take in a little spendin' money from these spo'ts, yere. When I score a goal on 'em I make two bits."

"Yes, but don't you have to pay it when they score on you?"

Waffle Jones chuckled. "That's only 'bout once in a coon's age," he answered.

Kilroy made decisions fast, and stuck by them when they were made. He liked the Southern boy's trim build and alert grin.

"Listen," he said. "I want you on the squad. Tell you what we can do. There's a room over my garage, and I need someone to look after the car and tend the furnace. That'll cover your board. I think I can get three other faculty members to give you their furnace jobs at two dollars a week. You'll be kept busy about three hours a day, but it won't come in the afternoon. What do you say?"

"Gosh," stammered Waffle. "You—you mean I can try fo' the team?"

"Just that," nodded Kilroy. "It won't be easy, because the season's nearly half gone. But you'll have your chance. Now go down and tell that druggist he's got to find a new soda clerk. I'll come along in the car and pick up your clothes."

That was on a Monday night. Wednesday, as the squad jogged off the field after heavy scrimmage, Coach Kilroy stopped his captain at the edge of the running track.

"Left side of the line holding better today?" he asked.

Barry Hughes nodded. "Looked so to me. Anyhow, they ought to," he grinned. "I spent nearly an hour showing Hartley how to swing his hips on the charge, when we're punting. It'll take an eel to get through him if he keeps on improving. Wiggins, at guard, is clumsier, but he takes up plenty of room."

"By the way," said Kilroy abruptly, "how's this new kid, trying out for the backfield?"

Hughes laughed. "Waffle Jones?" he asked. "I don't know much about him but he seems to be a character. He's in dead earnest—a typical Southerner, with lots of fight. He tackled Butch Davis pretty hard this afternoon and Butch was sore. Called the boy 'po' white trash' and Waffle came after him with both fists swinging. They'd have put on the Battle of Bull Run if I hadn't pacified 'em."

Kilroy frowned. "Hard tackling is all right," he said, "but we can't use hotheads. The scrub coach says

Jones is a fair blocker and he handles the ball as if he knew how. He may be too light, though, to be much good to us."

"Wait a minute," put in Hughes. "Have you seen him boot one? He's got a hind leg like a mule and he gets 'em off in nothing flat. I thought—" he hesitated—"I just wondered if he wasn't the quick-kicker we were praying for."

In the gathering darkness Kilroy grinned. So Barry Hughes was impressed, too! But that near fight—it wouldn't do, to let a feud grow up between Butch and Waffle.

That evening, while Waffle was washing the car, his new employer strode into the garage. He looked on a while in silence. Then, "Jones," he said suddenly, "they tell me you've got a temper. Good. I wouldn't give two cents for a man that didn't. But if you can't control it, there's no point in your going out for a place on my team."

Waffle tossed the sponge into the bucket and stood up, looking him in the eye. "Thank you, suh," he answered, reddening. "I'll sho'ly try."

He did try, manfully, but it wasn't always easy. Butch Davis, the first-string fullback, kept his grudge, and whenever chance brought them together in scrimmage, the big line-plunger scowled and put extra steam into his attack. He had decided that Waffle Jones was showing off—trying to make an impression. And with the blunt, hard-headed fullback, that didn't go down.

Once, when Butch was charging in to make a tackle and Waffle cross-blocked him out of the play, the Virginia boy felt a heavy knee drive home to the pit of his stomach. He staggered to his feet, fists clenched, eyes blazing. But with his wind knocked out, the fighting words died in his throat in a wheezing moan. And by the time he could speak, he had himself in hand.

The first Saturday in November, Jones sat happily on the bench, a big new 68 gleaming on the back of his maroon jersey. He was part of the Cameron squad. Any minute, now, the coach might catch his eye and shoot him into the game.

It didn't happen, however. Cameron walked through the Harley team for thirteen points in the first half, and unleashed a beautiful passing attack to score three more touchdowns in the second. The line held on punts, and only once did Butch Davis fail to get his kick away. That was on third down and a Cameron man recovered the ball, so no harm was done.

The Harley victory gave Cameron a record of six straight wins and no defeats—a Conference standing equaled only by the powerful State University team.

And the school's championship hopes burst into a flame that swept the campus.

The only game of the year outside the Conference was a contest with Harnell, to be played the following Saturday at Northville. Cameron had been scheduled as a breather for the Big Red team. Now, with the Maroon's impressive string of conquests in mind, the newspapers began to talk of a possible Cameron victory.

It was a hilarious crowd that gathered that Monday night after signal practice, for the weekly blackboard drill. But as always, when Hike Kilroy held up his hand the chatter died instantly.

"I guess," he said deliberately, "you've all been reading the sport pages. Don't let it go to your heads. We've got two games ahead of us that aren't in our class—Harnell and State. I'm going to ask you a question. If you had your choice between beating Harnell, Saturday, and beating State for the title, which would it be?"

"State!" shouted thirty voices simultaneously.

Kilroy nodded. "I think we can win one of those two games," he said. "I'll tell you frankly it would mean more to my reputation to trim Harnell. We could shoot the works, and possibly catch them off their guard. I've got a new play to give you that's a giant killer. But State will be scouting us Saturday. Now get me right. We're going up to Northville and fight. We'll win if we can. But it'll be with straight football and plenty of substitutes. We're not going to cripple the team or give away our best plays. We're pointing for State!"

"Yea-a-ay, Hike!" bellowed someone in the back of the room, and the whole squad echoed the cheer.

Kilroy lifted his hand again. "All right," he said. "Let's get down to brass tacks. Here's that new play we're going to start work on tomorrow. We'll call it number 91. It's a quick kick."

That week Waffle Jones found himself suddenly conspicuous. Out of the obscurity of the scrub, where he had been laboring without special distinction, he was elevated to the Varsity squad. Every afternoon he and Butch Davis were taken aside by the head coach for a fifteen-minute kicking drill.

The situation irked Butch. He couldn't understand why a raw rookie who had come on the squad late in the season should receive special attention. Why didn't he take his chances with the rest? Why all this grooming of an unknown? Waffle, on the other hand, gazed in open-mouthed admiration at the fullback's high, graceful spirals. His own punts looked ragged by comparison. They had length and speed but the ball usually flew end over end and wobbled erratically.

"Gosh," he exclaimed, "I sho' would like to kick thataway! How is it you hold 'em?"

"Here, Jones," the coach interposed sharply. "Don't you go fooling with spirals. Kick your own way, and remember all I want is speed and direction."

He tossed the ball to Red Landis, the center, who crouched above it, awaiting the signal to pass.

"This time," said Kilroy, "I want you closer to the line and over here to the left—the number three spot, in a double wing-back formation. Landis, you'll have to watch your pass. Keep it on his right, and waist high. I'm going to be the opposing tackle and block it if I can. All right—let her go!"

Waffle saw the ball shoot toward him, caught it at arm's length, and swung his foot, all in the space of a second. Then Kilroy's charge knocked him flat. By the time he regained his feet, the scrub quarter, who had been elected to catch and return punts, was running after a bouncing oval, far over in the corner of the field.

"You'll do," puffed Kilroy, with one of his rare smiles. "They'll never get through on you any faster than I did. And you placed it just right. Take a couple more for practice and we'll start scrimmage."

Flushed with pleasure, the Virginia boy stole a look

at Butch Davis. But the big fullback had turned on his heel and was walking away.

For ten thrilling minutes of the afternoon scrimmage, Waffle Jones was in the line-up of the Varsity. And twice during that time Hal Decker, at quarter, called the 91 signal. The first time, a bad pass from center dribbled off the Southerner's finger tips and he was forced to fall on the ball beneath an avalanche of scrub linemen. But the second try worked.

The team had the ball on its own 40-yard line, second down and four to go. The scrub secondary was in close, expecting a running play. Waffle got his kick away fast and the Varsity ends raced down the field under it. The scrub safety man was caught flat-footed. He turned, as the oval sailed over his head, and rushed back after it, but Moran touched it down five yards from the goal. Forced to punt, the scrubs lost twenty yards on the exchange, and a few plays later the first team put over a score.

Heading for the gym at a trot, when practice was finished, Waffle felt a big hand slap him between the shoulder blades.

"Nice work, kid!" said a friendly voice, and Barry Hughes jogged up beside him. "Don't worry about that wide pass. You won't get one in fifty like that from Red Landis. He's steady as a rock."

Thirty-five men entrained for Northville on Friday night, and Waffle was undoubtedly the proudest member of the party. He spent an hour or two Saturday morning strolling up and down the famous hills of the Harnell campus. Then the squad had an early lunch and rested till game time. It was a gray day, overcast and cold. After the warm-up, Waffle pulled on his hooded maroon jacket and took his place on the bench.

The game started slowly. It took the big Harnell machine a few minutes to thaw out. Then, just as their power thrusts off tackle began to work, Decker recovered a fumble, and a brilliant forward from midfield took the Red defense by surprise. Weasel Blake, catching it on the run, squirmed past the safety man and ran for a touchdown.

Foley, the Maroon's left halfback and star placement kicker, converted the point. And at the end of the opening period the score was 7-0 in Cameron's favor.

After that the aroused Harnell team gave them no more chances. Half a dozen times the Red attack swept down the field, only to be held by a fighting Cameron line in the shadow of the goal. Then one of Butch Davis' beautiful punts would take the ball back to midfield and the steam roller would start again.

It couldn't go on forever. Five minutes before the half ended a smashing crossbuck split the tiring Maroon forward wall, and Harnell scored. Promptly Kilroy took out the whole first line and sent them to the dressing room. And the reserves managed to avert another touchdown for the remainder of the period.

In the second half Cameron kept the offensive for a time, and even threatened the Red goal. Then the breaks went against the Maroon. A pass intended for Blake was intercepted and a Harnell back, running behind quick-forming interference, galloped to the Cameron 5-yard stripe before he was downed. Two sledgehammer blows at the line took the ball over. Harnell was leading by a touchdown.

The next kick-off was short, and a good runback gave Cameron the ball on its own 45-yard line. Waffle Jones began to fidget on the bench. He looked at Kilroy expectantly. The Red backs were drawn in. It was just the time for the 91 play. The coach glanced toward him with a shake of the head that was barely perceptible.

Decker knifed through on a spinner for three yards. Butch Davis plowed off tackle for two, tried again at center and made only inches. Then the big fullback dropped far to the rear and kicked a high spiral that fell neatly in the safety man's arms on the Harnell 20-yard line. Waffle gave a little groan. The chance was gone.

Cameron fought gallantly through the last quarter,

but always on the defensive. Kilroy began putting in substitutes. Waffle Jones saw the coach beckon and sprang to his feet. With a pounding heart he ran up and down the side line, then sprinted out on the field.

Those final minutes of the game were a nightmare of grueling punishment. Under the steady pounding, Cameron's reserves gave ground doggedly but inevitably. The young Virginian lost all track of yardage. All he knew was the desperate charge of the secondary to pile up a play that had pierced the line—the smash of his body across an interferer's legs—the clutch of his hands on a stained red jersey.

Once he saw a broad white stripe on the ground when he picked himself up. There must have been a touchdown, he thought dully. But he was being pounded on the back and a voice yelled, "It's a penalty! Harnell offside!" And then came the faint crack of a gun. The game, Waffle realized, was over.

As he stumbled toward the side line, someone threw a blanket around his shoulders. He was trotting with the squad toward the showers. "Say," he panted, as a big figure pulled abreast of him, "what was the score?"

Barry Hughes peered at him and laughed. "Fourteen-seven," he answered. "You were sure in there fighting, kid!"

Fourteen-seven. Then they had really held them—

stopped the Harnell attack with second stringers! He was proud of Cameron in defeat.

The whole squad got a rest on Monday. But Tuesday afternoon, in a drizzling rain, they went to work in earnest. The field was guarded that final week. Forty stalwart undergraduates patrolled the running track, with suspicious eyes for anyone resembling a stranger. And inside the cordon, Hike Kilroy cracked the whip over his squad. There were brief daily drills in fundamentals, but the work was concentrated on two or three new deception plays and the quick kick.

Waffle Jones was in the Varsity line-up most of the time, now. He tried to keep clear of Butch Davis, but the fullback's hostility was too open to be ignored. Once, when he was sent in at half in the middle of scrimmage, he saw Butch turn to Bill Ray, the right guard, and heard him say something about "—that po' white trash is in again!"

In a flash he stood before his enemy, fist drawn back and trembling. "When the season's over," he said, through clenched teeth, "I'll take that out o' yo' hide!"

Barry Hughes shouldered between them. "Shut up, kid," the captain growled, "and you too, Butch. Now get in there and play football!"

By Friday night the whole squad was down to a fine edge—not overtrained but restless and fidgety as a bunch of thoroughbreds at the barrier. In his room over the garage, Waffle Jones tried to do some studying, gave it up, went to an early picture show, and turned in at nine-thirty. For half an hour he tossed on his pillow, signals racing through his head, his muscles twitching with eagerness for battle. Then he dropped into a sound sleep and didn't wake till it was time to tend furnaces in the morning.

The campus was astir early. Old grads and pretty girls began to appear, and excited students cut their morning classes. Waffle lunched with the team and took a walk until it was time to dress. The players were gruff and silent in the locker room. At just the right moment, Hike Kilroy strolled in.

"Hi, gang!" he called cheerily. "Last game! No more black-and-blue practices. Just a swell afternoon for football, and a chance to prove you're as good as I think you are. Let's get the jump on 'em and play 'em off their feet!"

The tension was gone in an instant. Waffle felt a surge of warlike joy, and jumped to his feet with the rest. The squad laughed and thumped one another on the back.

There was a big crowd in the stands, cheering mightily as the vanguard of maroon jerseys trotted on the field. Three blue-clad State elevens were already snapping through their signal drill. They were big, all right. They outweighed Cameron ten pounds to the man, and looked it.

Waffle went through the warm-up in a sort of trance and woke up to find himself on the bench, with Barry Hughes and the State captain shaking hands in mid-field. There was little wind. State won the toss and chose to receive.

And the kick-off! It went to the fifteen, and Blue interference seemed to form by magic. Downed by right halfback Judd on the 35. The teams barely had time to crouch, when Craven, State's hard-running back, was racing around left end behind a flying cloud of blue. It took Decker, the safety man, to bring him down, and he was five yards past the center stripe.

Caught off balance, the Cameron team had hardly lined up before a crushing off-tackle thrust gained 20 yards more, and then a long forward settled in the arms of a State back for a touchdown.

The game was just a minute old and Cameron was six points behind. A moment later it was seven, as Craven converted the point with a placement.

Waffle sat stunned. The "jump" so important in a close game, had gone to the enemy. He wondered if it *would* be close.

State received again, and this time Jack Moran, down-field like an Irish whirlwind, slammed the great Craven in his tracks. The stands roared as Barry burst through on the first play to smother a runner behind the line. State fell back to kick and the game was under control once more.

The rest of the first period was a slam-bang battle. Cameron worked the ball into enemy territory twice, and on one occasion reached the Blue 20-yard line, but was held for downs by inches.

It was well along in the second period, and Coach Kilroy was beginning to steal glances at his watch, when Waffle heard Decker bark a signal, and watched, tense and breathless, as the play started. It was one of the new tricks. Cameron's ball on the State 35.

The oval went to Decker, then to Foley, and deftly back to Butch on a fake reverse. Butch put back his long arm and threw a low, swift pass that traveled twenty yards like a bullet.

Weasel Blake was in the clear—out to the right. He took one quick look over his shoulder, reached upward, and snagged the ball without losing stride. Two defense men raced across to cut him down. The first he shook off with a sidewise leap. The second brought him to earth a step short of the goal.

There was no holding Cameron then. Barry and Ray tore a hole in the State line, and Butch Davis went through the gap like a moose through a thicket. The teams lined up in front of the goal posts. Decker knelt to catch the placement. And just as the half ended, Foley's toe smacked it cleanly over to tie the score.

Through the frenzied yelling from the stands, the subs raced for the gym. Waffle Jones was standing just inside the door when the Varsity came in. He waited till Davis had settled wearily on a bench, then stole toward him.

"Say, Butch," he muttered lamely, "I just wanted to tell you—well—you were swell!"

The big line-plunger looked up at him without reply, frowned, and bent once more to retie his shoe laces. Reddening, the boy walked away. His eagerness was gone. He hardly cared whether Cameron won or lost. Then a hand slapped his shoulder and the friendly voice of Barry Hughes was asking how he felt.

"Going to pull old 91 on 'em, this half!" grinned the captain, as he lay back on the rubbing table.

"You bet!" said Waffle, and felt better.

Kilroy came in for the last three minutes. He talked quietly, without heroics, but there was an edge to his words. "All right," he finished. "Every man in every play. You've got the stuff to win this game."

It was obvious, as the second half started, that the State team had been given a tongue lashing. They tore in with a sullen ferocity that ruined Cameron's first two plays after the kick-off. Davis planted a long punt down the field. And then the bigger team's power attack started.

Smash, smash, smash at the line, and then a swinging end run behind interference that looked like a battery of tanks. First downs by inches—first downs by yards. Twice the Maroons stiffened to hold them and kick out of danger. But the third time State crashed over. On the try for point, Ray's headlong rush half checked the rising ball and it hit the crossbar to bounce back. No goal. State, 13; Cameron, 7.

That was still the score when they changed ends for the final quarter. There was swaggering confidence in every movement of the blue jerseys. They had a lead, and they had the Maroon ball carriers stopped.

Held on her own 30-yard line, Cameron punted. The State runback brought the ball nearly to midfield, and they started what looked like another touchdown march. Two downs and only a yard to go for first down. Then came a break—a little carelessness in the State backfield, and a fumble that rolled wide. Moran, the cruising ball hawk, was on it like a shot.

Even before the referee had untangled the pile, Waffle heard his name called. "Go in there, Jones, and do your stuff!" said Kilroy. "This is the spot."

Running across the field—giving up his substitute's slip—jumping into the left halfback position, Waffle felt numb with excitement. The signal called for a buck. Judd went through right guard for three yards. The ball was just over the center line, ten yards in from the left side of the field.

"Fifty-seven — ninety-one — forty-six — nine — eleven—" Hal Decker was barking.

Waffle saw the square, close defense of the State backs, braced himself, and caught the pass, rifled true into his hands by Red Landis. With the quick thud of his toe came a looming wave of Blue linemen, but the ball was away. As he scrambled to his feet he saw Weasel Blake swooping after the rolling pigskin, deep in the far corner of the field. Then he gave a startled gasp. The flying end checked his speed, waited till the ball bounced over the goal line, and flung himself on it just as the blue-clad pursuers reached him.

"Gosh!" choked Waffle in dismay. "Now it'll have to come out twenty yards!"

Decker was whooping, pounding him on the back. "Come out nothing!" cried the hilarious quarter. "Their safety man had his hands on it, and that crazy end-over-end kick of yours got away from him. It's a touch-down!"

WAFFLE HURLED HIMSELF FORWARD

On the scoreboard new numbers were posted: "State, 13; Cameron, 13."

They lined up. With Foley out, Butch would attempt the placement. "We've got to make this point—*got* to make it!" Waffle was telling himself feverishly. "Got to protect Butch's toe! He's slow!"

Just behind him and to the right he heard Hal Decker, down on one knee, yelping the signal. And suddenly he knew something was wrong. Hartley, the left tackle was hurt. Crouched there in the line, his back swayed uncertainly. At the instant the ball was passed he toppled sidewise, and through the wide-open gap came a State guard like a runaway locomotive. Waffle didn't wait for the charge. He met it— hurled himself forward with all the strength in his wiry body. There was a sickening smash, and daylight went out abruptly.

When he came to, it was raining—raining bucketfuls, it seemed. The water boy stopped showering him and grinned.

"Collar bone," a bearded man said, in a matter-of-fact tone.

They supported him between them and carried him off through a lane of anxious, friendly faces—the team! It wasn't till they reached the bench that he recalled what had happened. Then he tried to turn to see the scoreboard and felt a knife stab his shoulder.

"Doctor, suh," he asked humbly, "could yo' tell me about that last placement?"

"We made it," smiled the medico. "And Hartley's all right. Just a bump on the head. Now lie still. I'm going to set this."

The next thing Waffle remembered was a tremendous sound of cheering and the beat of marching feet. Then Hike Kilroy's rugged face was bending over him.

"Good work, Jones," said the coach. "If any man saved that game, you did! Here's a chap wants to tell you so."

And with that the boy found himself looking up at Butch Davis.

"You win, kid," said the fullback huskily. "When you're feeling like it again you can kick me all over the campus if you want to."

"Huh!" chuckled Waffle. "Reckon I don't want to. But I'll play yo' a game o' kickin' up an' down the field —two bits a goal!"

THE LONG, TALL DOGS OF KETTLE RIVER

THE BOX-CAR bumped and clattered over the switch-points and came to a jerking stop. There were voices outside in the frosty air—shouts and laughter—and Shawn McLeod pushed open the door a few inches to look out. Against the dark back-drop of the spruce forest he saw a sprawling town. A long, wide, snow-covered street, flanked by log shacks and ugly, square-fronted stores of raw lumber. It was Hennigan, the newest and richest of the Northern Ontario gold camps.

"Looks like we're here," Shawn said. And Paddy, straining at his chain, gave tongue in answer. His tremendous voice resounded shatteringly in the car. It was a deep, challenging roar, somewhere between a bark and a bay.

Shawn opened the door wide to admit the winter daylight and the sharp, biting cold. He picked up the racing-sled with care and deposited it outside in the snow. Then he went to unchain the dogs. All four of them had caught the contagion of excitement now. The clamor they raised was deafening.

He led Paddy to the door first, picking up the long tangle of dog-harness on the way. They jumped down together—the big leader and the lean, rangy boy—and Shawn held the chain with one hand while he deftly straightened out the harness with the other.

A group of onlookers had straggled over from the holiday crowd that milled in Hennigan's main street. There were white men and Indians—miners, trappers, lumberjacks, in bright plaid mackinaws and fur-hooded parkas.

A burly Frenchman watched Shawn buckle Paddy's neck into the front collar, between the trace-straps, and laughed.

"Trapper's hitch!" he remarked with scorn. "You t'ink for go in race lak dat?"

Shawn paid no attention. He was on his way back to the freight-car. Duke came next. Then Joker, and finally Rusty. The old, smoke-blackened dog-pail with its sack of corn-meal and whitefish, which accompanied him on all his journeys, was placed on top of Shawn's snowshoes on the sled. He took his position at the gee-bar and picked up his home-made whip with the long rawhide lash coiled around the stock.

"Hey, Buddy," a gray-bearded oldtimer cackled. "What fer Pete's sake kind o' dogs is them? Looks like ye'd crossed a cow moose with a timber-wolf."

Shawn nodded. "That's right," he said soberly. "You guessed it right off."

There was an appreciative guffaw from the spectators. "Got you that time, Sourdough! The kid ain't so dumb. Guessed it right off—haw! haw!"

Shawn started the sled with a shove. "Mush on!" he called and the tall dogs braced into their collars, trotting out of the railroad yard with the boy riding the sled-tails.

Amused comments followed him up the snowy street. "Look a' the sled, Mike! Did y'ever set eyes on the likes o' that? An' the dogs! Begob, they're wearin' stilts!"

Shawn guided his team through the throng and brought them to a stop in front of the Gold Nugget Hotel. That was where he had been told he would find the race committee. On the wall of the frame structure a crude poster was tacked up. "Hennigan Dog Derby," it read. "New Year's Day. $100 to the winner."

"Here's another one, Sandy!" someone shouted, and a big voice boomed in reply—"Bring him in!"

A giant of a man in a fur coat and cap was standing in the hotel doorway. Shawn addressed him diffidently. "Mr. Donaldson?"

"The same," replied the big man. "An' I take it you're Angus McLeod's lad, from Kettle River. We got your letter an' you're entered. Tell me one thing, though.

Where did a braw Scotsman like yourself come by the name o' Shawn. That's Irish, isn't it?"

"It is," said Shawn. "My mother was an O'Hara."

Big Sandy Donaldson looked into the boy's proud, unsmiling face and nodded gravely. "It's a hard mixture to beat in a fight," he said. "An' the dogs? I see there's only four o' them."

Curious, he was staring at the team. They were strange-looking brutes, gaunt, big-boned and rough-coated, with a shag of reddish hair over their eyes and around their muzzles.

"The dogs are like me," said Shawn. "Part Irish staghound an' setter—part Airedale." He grinned. "A hard mixture to beat in a fight—or anything else."

Big Sandy put back his head and roared. He was camp boss at Hennigan, and head of the committee in charge of the Derby.

"Did ye hear that, Mr. Carroll?" he asked over his shoulder. "Come here, lad, an' meet the owner o' the mines. Mr. Carroll, this here's Shawn McLeod o' Kettle River. Trapper, guide, an' now dog-driver."

Another fur coat appeared beside Donaldson's. The boy saw a short, smiling man with gray hair and crisp wrinkles around the eyes. "Heard of you," said Mr. Carroll as he shook hands. "New York friends of mine talk about the moose-hunting up Kettle River way. Like you to meet my daughter, Jean."

The little girl of ten who stepped forward looked to Shawn like some kind of winter fairy. Yellow curls clustered around her elfin face, and she wore a coat and cap of gleaming ermine. Shawn ought to know ermine when he saw it. He had sold more than fifty of the tiny white weasel pelts to the fur-buyer the week before.

He mumbled a greeting and bowed stiffly over the child's hand. "I'll have to get back to the team," he said. "Race is s'posed to start in twenty minutes."

He took hold of Paddy's collar and pulled him over to a snow-bank across the street. Other teams and mushers were gathered there. French Louis Paquet and his wolf-faced malamutes; Joe Wilton, from Cochrane, with his yellow-white Siberians; and half a dozen men he did not know. All kinds of dogs made up the teams, though the husky strain was most in evidence. Every minute or two a hideous din of snarling and growling would threaten a general fight, and only by constant vigilance did the drivers keep the teams from each other's throats.

Shawn had witnessed scenes like this before, but he had never felt the sick nervousness at the pit of his stomach that beset him now. It was his first race. When he had come home from his trap-lines to spend the holidays, two weeks before, he found the Hennigan Dog Derby was the chief topic of conversation. One of his father's Indian guides had mentioned that he knew how to build a racing sled. And the whole idea had taken form right then.

They had worked hard on that sled, bending it out of split birch, lashing it with moosehide thongs. It didn't look like much, now that Shawn compared it with the equipment of the other drivers, but he knew at least that it was strong. The "trapper's hitch," laughed at by the Frenchie, down at the track, was something that couldn't be helped. These lanky dogs of his were fast, but they had been broken since puppyhood to the straight tandem pull in double traces, used on the trappers' toboggans. The regular racing hitch was what all the other mushers were using. A long, single strap from the front of the sled to the leader's collar, with the rest of the team pulling on shorter thongs, fastened to either side of the trace. Five to seven dogs made up most of the teams.

A stockily built driver, whose black and white huskies lay resting in the snow next to Shawn's dogs, tossed away a cigarette and looked up at the gray sky. "Might be comin' on to storm," he remarked. "Too bad if it does. Trail's good and fast now. You been over it?"

"No," said Shawn. "I just got in on the train a few minutes ago."

"Most of it's good goin'," the other man told him. "About four miles up the river, this side, then cross over an' down. They call it twenty-five miles, countin' the three trips around. Only one bad hill an' a few mean turns in the trail . . ."

He was interrupted by a hoarse sound from his leader, and seized his collar barely in time to avert a lunge at the bristling Paddy.

"Must be you want to get cut up!" he reproved the husky. Then he stared again at Shawn's great brindled lead-dog and hastily edged away. "Gawsh—look at them teeth!" he muttered.

The boy moved from one dog to the next, settling the collars and back-straps in place, feeling of the buckles, testing the traces. He talked to the restless animals as he went. They were own litter-brothers and nearly alike in size and appearance, but each of the four had a personality of his own.

Paddy was the tallest and the steadiest—certainly the most intelligent. He had in him more of his grandsire, the mighty stag-hound, Brian Boru—brought from Ireland by Shawn's uncle. Duke was sedate and aloof, with the solemn brown eyes of an Irish setter under a shaggy fringe of brows. When Shawn came to Joker, the irrepressible scamp reached up to wipe his face with a great wet tongue. Joker was mischievous and lovable as an overgrown puppy, and the Airedale in him showed in his black saddle and crisp, rough fur. Rusty's coat had more of a reddish tinge than any of the others. He was powerfully built and businesslike. A born puller, always ready for the trail.

Across the street at the hotel, Sandy Donaldson's deep voice made itself heard. The drawings were about to take place, he announced. "An' to make it all square to everybody's satisfaction," he added, "we'll ask this little lady here to pull the numbers out o' the hat."

Laughing, the small girl in the ermine furs proceeded to draw. Joe Wilton's name came out first, and he led his Siberians proudly to the starting line. Behind him came Shawn's stocky neighbor, and in third place Louis Paquet, brave in a red blanket-cloth shirt. Shawn was drawn in fifth position among the seven starters.

It was a big field for a sled-dog race. Lined up for the start, one team behind another, they were strung out for more than a hundred yards along the street. There were several minutes of restless waiting while the committee checked the places and put a hundred-pound bag of sand on each sled. Shawn fidgeted, looked around for some possible familiar face in the crowd, stared at the leaden sky and wondered how much longer the snow would hold off. Down at the railroad track the little locomotive huffed and chuffed, hauling out on its return trip to Moose Lake Junction.

"All ready, there?" bellowed Sandy Donaldson. "Start with the gun!"

Four or five breathless seconds passed. At last a .44 revolver roared and the mushers sprang to their gee-poles as a tremendous shout went up from the crowd.

Shawn set the sled in motion with a push and a run. Then, as the dogs' eager pull tightened the traces, he swung lightly onto the ski-like tails of the sled-runners. The team of huskies behind him came up with a rush, trying to pass before the trail narrowed at the edge of town. Shawn rarely used a whip on his dogs and now there was no time to shake out the furled lash. He crouched lower over the back of the sled and sent a piercing cry through the general clamor. "Yippee, Paddy! Hi-up, Duke!"

The dogs stretched their long legs, pulling up on the sled in front, and the husky leader dropped back out of Shawn's line of vision. Up ahead he could see Louis Paquet's malamutes swinging wide to race past the second-place team. Then the last of the yelling crowd was behind them and the black spruce forest shut in like a wall on either side of the narrowing trail.

Shawn's dogs were running easily, with Paddy's nose

a scant five yards behind the tail of the next sled. The trail was over uneven ground, rough with bumps and hollows, but the firmly packed snow made the going fast. Shawn balanced himself on the runners, swaying to the pitch and heave of the sled. He had no plan except to hold his place and find out what the course was like.

It was impossible to see far along the trail because of its turns and twists. They had gone two or three miles before a straight vista opened up and Shawn caught a glimpse of a tiny red speck in the distance. Louis Paquet —that was. And he had a long lead on the third and fourth place teams. Too long!

Just ahead the trail widened a little. "Haw, there, Pat!" the boy shouted, and as the big dog swung obediently to the left, he lifted the whole team forward with a quick "Hi-up! Mush on!"

The other driver laughed, as Shawn's sled flashed by. "I'll be seein' you!" he called. "Them long-legged pups won't last!"

The young trapper had no time to answer. He was already overhauling the next team—driven by the man he had talked to before the race. As Paddy drew even with the sled, the burly musher whooped to his dogs and began pouring leather into their tossing backs. They picked up speed. Shawn might still have passed, but the wide place in the trail ended abruptly, and the rangy leader was forced to drop back once more.

A big, cold flake of snow landed on Shawn's cheek, and in a few seconds more the air was filled with them. The threatened storm had begun in earnest. The boy from Kettle River had mushed his team through falling snow too often to be worried by this development. The only thing that bothered him was the lack of a view ahead. It was impossible to see fifty yards through that blinding curtain of white. With one mittened hand he turned up the hood of his canvas parka. "Hup! Hi-up, there!" he encouraged the dogs.

The trail made a sharp bend to the right and led down to the river. There was a red bandanna handkerchief on a stick, set up on the shore. The turning mark for the course. Beside it crouched an Indian in a fur cap, making sure none of the mushers took a short cut. He waved to each driver as he went past.

The huskies ahead hit the level ice going like smoke, and Shawn had no chance to overtake them there as he had hoped. On the other side, the trail pitched sharply up the bank. He jumped off, pushing on the gee-bar, and helped the dogs over the crest. Then they were heading downstream again close on the heels of the third-place sled.

The snow beat into their faces in swirls and flurries.

It was increasingly hard to see. Right ahead, Shawn heard the sudden yelp of a dog and a stream of oaths from the driver he was following.

"Whoa, Pat! Whoa-up, Duke!" he shouted, and as the sled slackened speed he saw that his stocky friend had come down to a sharp turn too fast and split his team around a tree. They were in a beautiful tangle now—the lead-dog and two of his mates fighting in a snarl of trace-straps—the driver plying his whip in a rage.

Shawn ran forward and gripped Paddy's collar. The trail was blocked by the sled and the embattled huskies, but there was a three-foot opening between the trees to the left. The boy guided his team through the gap, the narrow sled following without mishap. They made a swift circuit around the other team and regained the trail beyond.

"Hi-up! Mush!" yelled Shawn, and jumped on the sled tail as it flew by.

There was nothing ahead to hold them back now, and the big dogs stretched out to run. They plowed into the storm at a steady lolloping gallop that ate up the miles. This was like many lonely journeys Shawn had made in his own Kettle River country. No living thing in sight. No sound but the muffled sigh of wind and hiss of snow. He clung to the gee-pole and peered through half-shut eyes into the gray whirl ahead.

After a while he heard a faint sound of cheering. One of the leading sleds must be passing through the town on its second lap. He shook out the long lash of his whip and cracked it venomously over the dogs' backs. "Get going, you, Pat! Hi—hi-up!"

He could feel the sled leap ahead. Twenty—thirty—forty seconds, and the first log shacks of Hennigan were in sight on the far bank. The team raced across the river and swung into the main street, lined on both sides with excited men. A gathering wave of sound swept them along. Shawn pointed ahead and tried to make himself heard. "How far? How far are they?" he cried.

The stragglers at the farther edge of town understood him at last. " 'Bout a minute!" one of them answered. "Go get 'em, kid!"

A minute. That meant a quarter of a mile or less, if the guess was correct. Shawn watched the steady rise and fall of the four snowy backs in front of him and felt a surge of exultant pride. They were good—this team of his!

It was snowing harder all the time, and a four-inch blanket of light, new flakes already covered the trail. The dogs began to slip a little, and slowed up on the rising ground. Shawn ran behind and beside the sled more than he rode. At the crossing, up-river, he called to the Indian, huddled beside his flag. "How much lead?" he asked.

The man grinned and pointed to the opposite shore, a hundred yards down. It was impossible to see that far, but the boy thought he heard the ghost of a shout —one of the mushers urging on his team. Then he was across, and the dogs were panting up the steep bank.

With the snow deepening constantly all the way down the back trail, Shawn left the rear of the sled and ran in front of the team. He had his second wind now, and jogged along as tireless as a young moose. The tall grandsons of Brian Boru followed him, strong and steady. In places where the wind had an open sweep the drifts were a foot and more in depth, but the rangy brutes pulled through them without slowing.

Shawn wondered how the shorter-legged malamutes and Siberians were taking it. They had stamina, he knew, and with seven dogs to the team, their individual loads were lighter. But by now their deep-furred bellies must be dragging a leaden weight of snow.

When he entered the camp's main street at the start of the final lap, the crowd was too busy watching the battle of the two leaders to cheer for him. He could see them now, a hundred yards ahead, flogging their teams neck-and-neck in a desperate race to be first out of town. Shawn's whip was back on the sled and he was still running in front of his dogs.

Remembering that he had eight miles yet to go, the boy saved himself as much as he could on the up-river stretch. Part of the way he rode the sled and let the dogs plow along at an easy pace in the trail already broken by the leaders. With the snow constantly deepening, he knew the real struggle would come in the last two or three miles.

Up at the turn he saw snowshoe tracks mingling with the marks of the sleds. One of the other drivers—whichever one was leading now—had started breaking trail. Rested, Shawn jogged forward to take his place in front of the team.

Half a mile down the last stretch he came on Joe Wilton, cutting away hard cakes of snow from his white leader's chest and legs. The dogs were all lying down, spent and gasping. The young Cochrane musher worked in a frenzy of haste, slashing away with his hunting-knife. He gave Shawn a black scowl as he went by. "All right—you break trail awhile an' see how you like it!" he panted.

Soon the boy came over a rise and saw Paquet's red shirt ahead. The Frenchman was laboring through a drift, his tired malamutes wallowing behind him. The man had no snowshoes, Shawn realized. He was wading knee-deep.

Shawn turned and motioned to Paddy to halt. Instantly the four dogs lay down in their traces, long red tongues hanging, trustful eyes on their master. He went back to the sled and pulled his snowshoes out from under the sand bag. As soon as they were on his feet he strode forward again. "Hup, boy! Mush on!"

Four or five minutes later they overtook Paquet's sled.

"Hey!" Shawn called. "Want to let me through? I'll break for you."

The French driver plodded on a few steps, then stopped and sullenly waved his young rival past. Shawn grinned. He was in the lead at last! A surge of new strength flowed through his wiry frame as he swung forward into the unbroken drifts.

For the next mile he set a pace that kept the dogs at a trot behind him. After that it was a matter of grim endurance. The thickly falling snow hid the landmarks along the trail and he had no idea how much farther he had to go. Over his shoulder he could see the wolfish heads of Paquet's malamutes close behind his own sled, and farther back he could hear Joe Wilton urging his team along. He knew they had comparatively easy going where he had packed the trail. Perhaps he should have waited—let them wear themselves out—

A sudden break in the swirling white showed him the shadowy shape of a house. He was coming into Hennigan. The trail dipped to the river crossing and he lumbered into a run. There were shouts behind him and howls and cheers in front. Up ahead he could see the roadway, trodden smooth and hard by hundreds of milling feet. The crowd was separating, forming a lane to the finish mark.

Floundering through the last drift, Shawn stopped to rip off his snowshoes. "Come on—mush!" he panted to the dogs, but a triumphant yell drowned his voice. Louis Paquet swept by, whip cracking, the malamutes at full gallop.

Shawn's hopes crashed. He was beaten by his own strategy. Bitterly ashamed, he was ready to quit right there, but he had forgotten the battling instinct of the dogs from Kettle River.

Paddy lunged forward like a brindled streak, jerking the others after him. By a desperate leap the boy managed to seize the gee-bar and swing himself onto the flying runners. He couldn't get at his whip, but no whip was needed now. The dogs were going with all the speed of their long legs, eating up the yards between them and the sled ahead. Shawn crouched low to cut down wind resistance and hung on for dear life.

The big leader's outstretched head flashed by the red-shirted Frenchman, then passed the malamutes one after another. With the finish a bare hundred feet away he pulled up abreast of the other lead-dog. Paquet was screaming, swearing, lashing his animals with cruel cuts of the whip. But the team from Kettle River stayed ahead.

They crossed the line a good two yards in the lead and were halfway out of town before Shawn could bring them to a stop. Louis Paquet had already turned and was some distance ahead of him when he swung the panting dogs back toward the hotel. That was why he failed to see exactly what happened next.

The crowd had poured out to fill the roadway with gesticulating, shouting figures. There hadn't been such a finish in a generation of sled-dog racing. They made boisterous way for the returning teams. "Tough luck, Frenchie!" they roared good-naturedly. "You darn near had him! Where is that kid? Here he comes!"

At that instant a high-pitched shriek cut through the babel of sound. Shawn saw the mob turn and push toward a common center in front of the hotel. He ran forward, seized Paddy's collar, and shouldered his way through till he could get a view of what was going on. Big Sandy Donaldson towered in the middle of the press, pushing men away with one arm. With the other he held up a limp little figure in an ermine coat.

"Bit her!" a man beside Shawn was saying excitedly. "That malamute lead-dog o' Frenchie's. She tried to pat him an' he got into her arm an inch deep!"

The half-wolf lay in the snow and took the savage beating Paquet was giving him without a yelp. Big Sandy and the child's father turned and carried her into the "Gold Nugget."

Outside in the street the race was almost forgotten. The miners and woodsmen talked over the accident in lowered voices. "It ain't anything to fool with—a bite like that," Shawn heard one of them say. "Oughta be 'tended to, but the camp doctor's gone to Ottawa for the holidays."

The other drivers came dragging in off the trail. One after another they asked who won, heard the story and stared curiously at the big brindle dogs curled up in the snow. At the end of twenty minutes, Donaldson came outside.

"Listen!" he boomed. "I want it quiet here so I can talk. Mr. Carroll's little girl has got a bad wound— maybe dangerous. We've done what we can, but she's got to get to a hospital. The spur-line engine at the junction blew a cylinder-head this mornin'—can't get back here. An' the Limited's due there at four-thirty.

We've got two hours an' a half to get the kid out to Moose Lake. Ten miles. Any musher here want to try it?"

There was a heavy silence. Louis Paquet's face was puckered with honest distress. "Me—I'd go queeck," he mumbled, "—on'y my dogs won' mush no more. Dat leader—she's done. W'en I lick 'im I bus' reeb, I t'ink, me."

The other drivers shifted uneasily, looked into the whirling whiteness and shook their heads. Big Sandy's face darkened. "What the devil!" he exploded. "Don't you know this may be a matter o' life an' death?"

Shawn was putting the snowshoes on his weary feet. "Anybody got a toboggan?" he asked. "It'll be better for this deep snow than a racin' sled."

Donaldson's huge hand descended on his shoulder in what was meant to be a pat of approval. "I'll get her ready," he told the boy. "Here, though—I 'most forgot." He pulled some bills out of his pocket and counted them into Shawn's mitten. "Ninety—ninety-five—a hundred," he finished. "An' you sure deserved to win. Too bad this had to happen. We'd have put on a celebration for you."

They lashed the Carrolls' suitcases on the old toboggan that a local trapper had produced. Then, while Shawn made fast the traces, Donaldson placed little Jean on the sled, with the luggage for a back-rest. Swathed in fur robes and blankets, she looked up and smiled courageously at the young driver. "This is going to be fun," she said.

Shawn moved slowly along the line of dogs. They were gaunt from the hard going of the morning, but their heads were up. Big Paddy looked at his master questioningly, his long tail waving with a slow grace.

"All right," said Shawn, "we better get goin'." He strode out ahead to break trail. Behind him trotted the team, and Mr. Carroll, on a pair of borrowed snowshoes, brought up the rear.

"I'll 'phone the agent at the junction again," Donaldson called after them. "He might be able to hold the Limited a few minutes, in a case like this."

Shawn led the way down to the railroad track, where the snow lay more than a foot deep over the ties and rails. The right-of-way was the shortest route to Moose Lake. There was a louder howl in the wind now—a savage sound coming down out of the northern wastes. The boy pulled the parka hood close about his face and leaned into the stinging blast. Four miles an hour was a killing pace, breaking trail, but he knew he had to do that and better to reach Moose Lake ahead of the train.

The snow was drifting badly. In some places the roadbed had been swept bare, and in others there were high mounds and ridges of shifting white. Shawn plowed on without slackening, picking up his heavy snow-shoes and putting them down. After what seemed hours of it, he saw a half-buried mile-post beside the track. It bore the number "5." He stopped then, and shouted back to the mine-owner, toiling along in the wake of the sled.

"What time is it?" he called hoarsely.

Carroll looked at his watch. "Twenty after three," he answered. He was breathing hard, and his face looked haggard. Shawn's respect for him increased. Any tender-foot who could do five miles on snowshoes, at the rate he had been going, was no quitter. "You want to rest an' ride the sled a while?" he asked.

The man shook his head. "Slow the dogs up too much," he panted. "I'll make it."

Shawn's own back and legs were aching with fatigue, and he knew how tired the dogs must be. They had lain down at once when he stopped. Now, at his brief command, they floundered to their feet again and strained into their collars.

On and on and on. Shawn lost track of mile-posts and of time. He only knew that he staggered forward and the dogs came after him. When he looked back he could see Mr. Carroll's lurching figure, far behind in the dim blur.

SHAWN STRODE OUT AHEAD TO BREAK TRAIL

The early northern night was shutting down. In the woods it would already have been too dark to travel, but there was still light enough in the narrow railroad cut for Shawn to keep on moving. After a time the dragging ache in his legs seemed to go away. His only sensation was one of effortless gliding, as if his body had no weight. A drowsy feeling of peace settled over him. So easy to go this way . . . through the air . . . why hadn't he thought of it before. . . .

He found himself suddenly awake again. He was lying on his side in the snow, and a hand was shaking his shoulder. Painfully he started up, found his snowshoes still on his numb feet, and somehow scrambled erect. As he stood swaying there in the half-dark, the sound of an urgent voice brought him back to full consciousness.

Mr. Carroll was tugging at his arm. "McLeod!" he pleaded. "Can't stop here! Look—isn't that a light?"

Shawn rubbed his eyes. Somewhere ahead there was a faint yellow glow wavering through the rush of snowflakes. "Yes," he croaked. "I'm all right now. We'll keep goin'."

He turned to the team. "Come on, Paddy. Hup, there, Duke! Mush on!"

The dogs climbed stiffly to their feet, shaking off the snow. The traces tightened and the toboggan moved again. Shawn plodded up and over the crest of a drift, his eyes fixed on that dim glow of light. How far away it was, he could not tell. Sometimes he was not even sure he saw it. Then, when the storm lifted for a moment, it stared at him suddenly like a blurred yellow eye. Another, smaller light moved beside it—a swinging speck that must be a lantern. He heard the faint sound of a hail and tried to answer, but the wind drove his voice back into his throat. He quickened his pace to a stumbling run.

The lantern came nearer and he could see the man carrying it. "Train gone yet?" he gasped, as they approached each other.

"No," shouted the station agent. "She's an hour late, 'count o' the snow. I got the engineer o' the dinky to turn on his headlight so's you could see. Say—you're all in! Can you make it?"

"Yes," said Shawn. "You better take a look at Mr. Carroll, though."

He plowed on into the glare of light from the spur-line engine, passed it, and reached the station platform. Down the main track to the west a long whistle quavered and another headlight pierced the snow. Men came out of the station-building. They lifted the little girl from the toboggan and helped Mr. Carroll take off his snowshoes. By the time the Limited had clanked to a stop, they were ready to go aboard.

The mine-owner came over to Shawn, a smile on his tired face. "Well, son," he said, "we made it—thanks to you and the dogs. She'll be at the hospital in Toronto in the morning. I guess you know I'll never forget this. Here—I've got to get on the train. Good-by till next summer. I'll be up for the fishing."

He clasped the boy's hand quickly and climbed the car steps. When the train had started, Shawn felt something in his chilled fingers, and looked down, dumbfounded, to see a hundred-dollar United States note.

The station agent slapped him on the shoulder. "Well, kid, I bet you could do with some rest! An' how about a big mug o' hot coffee?"

"Swell!" Shawn grinned. "But first I'd like to feed these dogs. I've got their grub right here on the sled—if I could use your stove a minute—"

He mixed the corn-meal mush—a whole pail of it—and threw in a whitefish apiece for the four of them. While it cooked, he made the dogs comfortable in the baggage-shed and carried spruce boughs from the woods back of the station to bed them down.

They were up again to greet him, when he returned with the warm food. Up again on shaking legs, stretching their chains, voicing their eagerness in little growls and whimpers.

Even now the code had to be observed. Paddy first—then Duke, Joker and Rusty, in proper order. They wolfed the food in great starved gulps, then sank down, each one with a sigh of content, on the spruce tips.

Tired as he was, Shawn took the time to stroke their heads and scratch the rough, wet fur behind their ears. "Good dogs," he nodded to them soberly. "You earned your grub today—and tomorrow we'll ride home in style to Kettle River."

The four brindled tails moved gently in answer. The big, yellow-brown eyes looked up at him, filled with a deathless devotion. If the young boss said it was good, everything was all right.

THE CURLY-NOSE SKATES

"THINGS work out in queer ways," Brad Townsend's mother used to say. "If it hadn't been for that old pair o' skates with the curly toes, an' the way Brad an' the Jenkins boy always got on like a couple o' strange dogs, chances are the Danford bank robbery'd never have been cleared up, an' Mary Sue, here"—pointing to her active young daughter—"might still have been sittin' in a wheel-chair!"

.   .   .   .

To Bradley Townsend, Caterwaul River was as familiar as the bed he slept in or the weatherbeaten farmhouse where he lived. It came brawling down a narrow valley along the south side of Hog Back Mountain, rippling over stones, plunging into deep black pools. Except at a few places where it widened out and ran quietly through lonely meadows it was simply an overgrown brook that scarcely deserved the name of river. Ever since he could remember, Brad had fished the trout pool below Indian Rock and gone swimming at the old mill-dam. The winding bank itself formed the southern boundary of his mother's land.

At fifteen he was as tall as most men, and lean and wiry from hard work. There were three of them in the family—Mrs. Townsend, courageously trying to keep a roof over their heads on the stony little hill-farm; Mary Sue, Brad's black-eyed tomboy sister, aged nine; and Brad himself.

The boy milked four cows night and morning, cut the wood, plowed, planted, and helped get in the crops. In winter he went to school, but by now he had gone as far as the one-room schoolhouse on the mountain could take him.

There was much excitement at the Townsends' on the September morning when Brad first set out for Danford High School. It meant early rising, for the town was four miles away, over a rutted country road. The family's one horse was needed on the farm, so Brad walked the distance, lunch-pail in hand.

The big country boy felt shy and awkward as he sat through his classes that day. The well-dressed youths and girls around him watched him with amusement and giggled at his discomfiture. Brad was red with embarrassment, but he returned their glances with a level eye.

At noon he retired to a fence corner and ate his meal undisturbed, for as a rule the town pupils went home to lunch. But when school was over, he found a group of boys waiting for him in the yard. Most of them were third-year students—older than he. They gathered around him, quite obviously bent on having some fun.

"Ah, there, hayseed," said Riggs Jenkins, son of the local feed and grain merchant, "got your 'taters all in?"

Loud laughter greeted this sally, and Brad grinned without replying.

"Whar be yew from, neighbor?" queried Jenkins, encouraged to continue.

"From the mountain," Brad muttered, "—up on Caterwaul River."

Cheers and cat-calls mingled with more laughter. And just then Brad saw one of his tormentors glance snickering at the ground behind him. Quickly he took a step to one side and found a boy crouching just back of where he had stood. At the same moment someone made a grab for his cap.

Brad took it off and put it in his pocket. He laid his books and lunch-pail on the grass, removed his coat and folded it on top of the pile.

"Now," he said, cheerfully, "I guess you boys want to find out if I'm any good. All right, one at a time. Who's the first?"

The snickers died down but no one came forward. Brad looked at Jenkins. "You had the most to say," he urged. "Why don't you talk some more?"

The big Junior's pink and white face flushed angrily. "Don't get smart, Freshman," he said. "I'll talk when I please." And he strode up to Brad in his best bullying manner. He was a tall, beefy fellow, with little pig-eyes and a selfish mouth. "See?" he finished, thrusting his jaw close to Brad's face.

The mountain boy made a sudden businesslike movement. His right arm whipped around Jenkins' neck and he whirled, gripping tight and twisting downward. It was no more than a simple headlock, executed with speed and decision. In another second, the stocky town lad was flat on his back, with Brad braced firmly across him. For a little while Jenkins floundered powerfully but to no effect. Then Brad heard another boy's voice above him. "You're down, Riggs. He threw you fair. Now get up like a man and shake hands."

Brad released his hold and rose. The boy who had spoken stood beside him. He was a pleasant-faced youngster with snapping gray eyes. "My name's Lin Kennedy," he said, offering Brad his hand. "Glad to know you, Townsend. Now come on, Riggs, and shake on it. I'm going to buy the two of you a soda."

Shamefaced, the grain dealer's son got up and put out his hand in sullen compliance. There was no friendship in his grip. Brad put on his coat and picked up the books and lunch-pail. "Thank you just the same," he said bashfully, "but I'd better be hikin' for home. I've got the chores to do."

"No, sir!" said Kennedy positively. "You come on. It won't take five minutes." And after a moment's hesitation Brad accepted. He liked Lin Kennedy instinctively.

They strolled along the sidewalk as far as the Farmers' and Merchants' Bank and were about to cross over to the drug store opposite, when Jenkins pointed to a big, shiny sedan, parked in front of the bank. The engine was idling smoothly. A man in a black felt hat slouched behind the wheel, puffing a cigarette.

"Your dad buying a new car?" asked Jenkins. "I never saw that one 'round here before."

"No," said Kennedy. "That's a strange machine. New Hampshire license plates, but they're so spattered with mud you can't read 'em."

The man at the wheel had stopped smoking and watched the three boys intently while they crossed the street. There was a drowsy silence in the September afternoon. An occasional car rattled past. Horses, hitched in front of the stores, switched at flies and dozed in the sun. Settled on a stool before the soda fountain Brad sipped his drink and looked over toward the bank once more. "Funny, isn't it?" he said. "The wheels of that car are clean enough—not a speck of mud on 'em. What do you suppose—"

His words were interrupted by a sudden sound. A muffled report, loud as the back-fire of a truck, but different. And almost before the boys could jump to their feet, grim drama woke the sleepy town.

Out of the bank vestibule walked a man with a sawed-off shotgun. He looked up and down the street, stepped down and opened the rear door of the car. Behind him were two more men carrying between them a heavy-looking iron-bound box. And after them came a fourth, also holding a shotgun from which a wisp of smoke curled. He was walking backward and covering the bank door. Within a space of perhaps ten seconds the men had taken their places in the car, and it leaped away from the curb with a roar of unleashed power. Only then did the shouting start, and people began to run out into the street. A parting shot from the rear of the bandit car rattled off a sidewalk sign and grazed a horse which screamed with fright.

Brad rushed out with the others. Lin Kennedy's face was white and wild-looking. "My dad—" he gasped, "if they shot him—" And Brad realized for the first time that the boy must be a son of old Hiram Kennedy, the bank's president. They sped across to the marble vestibule. Inside the cool, dark banking-room there was confusion. Two clerks were stooping above a huddled figure in a corner. Someone was telephoning the police in a loud, frightened voice.

Then from an office at the rear of the bank, a tall white-haired man came, hat in hand. "Gee, Dad!" Lin Kennedy cried, with a choke of relief, "you're safe!"

"Yes," said the banker quietly, "they got poor Jones, the cashier, though. His left shoulder's nearly shot away. And they got all the cash—thirty-four thousand dollars. I'm going after them with the chief."

At that moment there was the shrill call of a siren outside, and the boys saw three policemen in a red roadster flash up to the curb. Close behind was an ambulance. Other cars were coming to life with a grind of starters and a crash of gears. As the bank president took his place beside the chief, men armed with guns and revolvers came running out of the hardware store and piled into waiting machines. And in an incredibly short time the posse was off on the robbers' trail.

.   .   .   .

Excitement was still running high in Brad's veins as he climbed the narrow, sandy road toward home. What a day it had been! He wondered if the news of the bank robbery had reached the mountain. It was quiet up there. Nothing much ever happened. Wouldn't the neighbors stare when they heard what he had seen?

The farm was in sight now. There was Mary Sue bringing home the cows. He saw them coming down in single file to the open bars across the road. Brad gave his high-pitched war whoop and waved to his sister, then broke into a run. Suddenly behind him a horn shrieked. As the boy jumped sidewise out of the road, a big sedan shot by. Through the dust he caught sight of three men crouching low in the rear seat. It was the bandit car!

The cows were crossing the road up ahead. Brad saw Mary Sue look up, startled, then dash out to drive old Daisy from the path of the oncoming car. There was a sickening instant as the huge machine lurched to the left, righted itself, then plunged with a crash into the trunk of the big rock-maple tree beyond the door-yard.

Brad ran on, stumbling, his brain numb with fear, for there in the road lay a pitiful little heap in blue gingham. His mother was kneeling at the girl's side when he got there. Mary Sue's eyes were open and she was breathing, but she did not know them. Tenderly Brad put his arms around her and carried her to the old couch on the porch.

"We've got to get a doctor up here quick," he said. "I'll run to Merton's an' telephone." Then he checked himself, remembering the gunmen in the car. Should he leave his mother alone? But as he stood, undecided, the problem settled itself. Brad heard the deep roar of an engine and another car came tearing up the road. He ran out, waving his arms and pointing to the wreck, and the red roadster pulled to a sudden stop.

Two policemen sprang out of the rumble seat and approached the smashed car warily, revolvers in their hands. There was an ominous silence as they drew near. Then a bareheaded man with blood streaming down his face rose out of the debris and put his hands above his head.

"All right," he croaked, "we're through."

One by one the police hauled three injured bandits from the car, searched them and took away their guns. The driver had been killed in the crash.

"Where's the other man?" asked the chief. "There were five of you."

"We threw him out, back in the woods, there," said the spokesman sullenly. "One o' you guys got him through the head."

"That's the one you thought you'd hit down on the Riverdale road, Charlie—before they doubled back," the chief remarked to one of his men. "All right, boys, you keep 'em here till we 'phone for a bigger car."

Hiram Kennedy had been making a search of the bandit machine during this time. Now he returned, and there was a worried frown between his eyes. He drew the chief a little to one side. "That cash-box isn't in the car," he said. "They must have stopped some-where and hidden it when they figured we had them trapped."

"But great guns!" exclaimed the policeman. "Don't seem as if they'd had time. We weren't more'n two or three miles behind 'em anywhere."

"My only guess is they got rid of it when they stopped to ditch that fifth man."

"H'm," said the chief, "maybe. Or it might be he wasn't hit at all—an' they turned the box over to him to make a get-away. Let's get back there an' start a hunt."

Brad had been standing close by and now he touched the big policeman's arm.

"They ran over my little sister," he said, "and she's hurt—bad, I guess. Could I go with you as far as the nearest telephone and try to get a doctor?"

The two men looked at the boy's drawn face and it was the banker who answered.

"You come right along, son," he said. "We'll get the best doctor in Danford. Never mind the cash-box. We'll hunt for that later."

And as they climbed into the roadster he turned a grim glance in the direction of the three bank-robbers. "Those devils did a pretty thorough day's work," he said, "but I reckon they're going to pay for it."

For four days little Mary Sue lay white and still, mercifully unconscious most of the time. Then she rallied. The doctor, who had spent hours each day at the Townsend farm, watched her open her lips in a tired smile and nodded approvingly. But when he left, his face was grave. "She'll pull through," he told Mrs. Townsend, "but she may be crippled for a long, long time. In fact, it's doubtful if she can ever walk again. It's her spine that's injured."

As the days shortened and the woods put on their autumn colors, Brad and his mother watched the child gain slowly and did everything they could to ease her pain. Little by little her old cheeriness came back, but not the color to her cheeks nor the strength to her legs. She still sat, like a little pale ghost, in a rocker by the window and waved good-by to Brad each morning as he started off to school.

He had made many friends among the boys in town. Lin Kennedy urged him to come out for the football team. Of course his farm-work at home made it impossible, but he was pleased to feel that they wanted him.

Gradually, the excitement over the bank-robbery had subsided. The body of the fifth bandit had been found in a wooded gully a hundred yards from the road, and the three surviving members of the gang had been brought to trial and duly sentenced to long prison terms. But one element of mystery still remained. No clue to the whereabouts of the bank's cash-box had been found, despite a systematic search along the roads and through the woods. And no amount of police threats or questioning by the prosecution had been of any avail in wringing the answer from the robbers. Somewhere between the Riverdale town-line and the crest of Hog Back Mountain, thirty-four thousand dollars in cash and securities was lost.

Few people in the township could forget the fact, for on trees and poles everywhere blazed red placards:

$1000

Reward

for information leading to recovery of an iron-bound box containing money and securities to the value of $34,496.60, stolen from this bank on Sept. 8

Farmers' and Merchants' Bank
of Danford, N. H.

For weeks every boy within ten miles spent his spare time ranging the countryside in an effort to find the treasure. A favorite spot was the stretch of woods between the road and Caterwaul River near where the dead robber's body had been located. There were even some sporadic attempts to drag the stream-bed, but all efforts proved fruitless. After a while even the optimists gave up the hunt.

When the heavy frosts of late November came, Brad found the daily hike to school more difficult. The road was frozen in hard ruts and ridges that slowed his pace. It was during a recess while he watched the skaters on the mill-pond behind the school that he thought of a better way to make his daily journey. The Caterwaul, he knew, was frozen almost all the way down to its juncture with the big river, just outside the town. Outside of two or three places where he might have to cut around the rapids, he could skate the whole distance. There was one big difficulty in his idea. Though he had learned to skate when he was seven, he had long since outgrown his first pair of skates, and for the last two years he had not been on the ice.

"Mother," Brad asked, that night, "could I have three dollars? If I could get a pair of skates I'd be able to make the trip to town in half an hour."

He saw her hesitate, her face sober, and pressed his point. "Gee," he said, "just think—I'd be home in time to get a lot more work done. Wouldn't that help?"

Slowly she shook her head. "I wish I could give it to you, Brad," she answered. "Goodness knows you've earned it. But we're going to need every cent." She looked toward Mary Sue in her chair by the window, and lowered her voice. "When the doctor was here yesterday," she said, "he told me there was only one way to cure her. That would be an operation by a big specialist in Boston. And it would cost four or five hundred dollars—with the hospital and all. I've figured if we save as hard as we can, we might get that much together in two years."

Brad nodded. "All right," he said, "I'll forget the skates."

But his mother didn't forget them. That evening he found her with a lantern, rummaging through an old trunk in the attic. As he drew near, there was a clinking sound of metal, and she stood erect, triumphantly holding up two curious objects.

"What under the sun—" Brad began.

"Skates!" said his mother. "It's a pair your father had, years an' years before you were born. I had an idea I'd seen 'em some place, an' here they are."

He took the things in his hands and tried to look as delighted as he knew she expected him to be. Yes, they were skates, Brad decided. But what skates! They had bodies of hand-whittled hickory, slotted at heel and toe to hold crumbling leather straps. And firmly fastened underneath were runners of ancient, rust-specked steel that curved up at the forward end in a sort of quaint scroll.

Brad's mother smiled happily as she closed the lid of the trunk. "Your Pa was a wonderful skater when he was your age," she said. "And he used to think a heap of those skates. I guess they'll be fine when you fix 'em up."

"Sure," Brad answered, with forced heartiness. "Just the thing." He took them downstairs and furtively tried one on his foot. The strap came apart in his hand as he attempted to buckle it. However, there were plenty of odd bits of harness in the barn. Before bedtime, he had succeeded in fitting stout new leathers in the slots, and had sand-papered off most of the rust. Then he started to file the cutting surfaces, and to his surprise he found the runners made of keen, hard steel.

At eight o'clock next morning, he sat on a log at the edge of the little river, and strapped the old skates tight over his cowhide shoes. They felt awkward when he stood up on them, and the ridiculous curling snouts in front looked as if they would get in his way. But by the time he had taken half a dozen strokes he knew that at least they would serve his purpose. He liked the way the sharp edges bit the ice, and they gave him a smooth run at the end of each stroke. Best of all, he discovered that his ankles were strong and he had lost none of his speed.

He made good time till he came to Piney Reach. There the water ran smooth and swift in a straight stretch of half a mile between black pine woods. The weather had not yet been cold enough to freeze this part of the river, and only a thin shell of ice showed at either bank. Brad took off his skates and walked along the shore till he came to strong ice beyond. From that point on it was fair skating all the way into Danford.

It was still a few minutes before school time when the lanky mountain boy reached the mill-pond. Among the dozens of students gathered on the ice, it was Riggs Jenkins who first caught sight of Brad and his skates.

"Whee!" he yelled. "Look at Caterwaul! Look at the sleigh-front skates!" And he swept past in a long glide, pointing with his hockey-stick. Others approached at the shout, and Brad found himself the center of a group of boys and girls, all convulsed with merriment at the sight of the quaint contrivances strapped to his feet.

"Did a set of sleigh-bells come with 'em?" asked Jenkins, fairly outdoing himself in sarcasm.

Brad grinned. "I admit they aren't so much to look at," he said, "but they can get over the ice. Guess maybe they can move as fast as those fancy ones you're wearin'!"

"Yeah?" sneered the town boy, unable for the moment to think of any other reply. The laughter of the onlookers shifted to him.

"How about it, Riggs?" someone called. "Aren't you goin' to stick up for those fifteen-dollar racin'-skates you've been braggin' about?" Cries of "Race! Race!" came from other quarters, and Jenkins looked around in annoyance.

"All right—I'll race him," he said angrily. "Any time—any place." The school bell started to ring as he spoke. "How about this noon?" a bystander suggested.

Brad shook his head. "I've got to go downtown an' buy medicine for my sister at noon," he said.

"Huh!" snorted Jenkins. "I thought he'd try to get out of it." And the matter was allowed to drop as they hurried toward the school building.

.   .   .   .

That night it turned cold. When Brad finished milking he paused a moment by the thermometer outside the shed door and saw the mercury slipping toward the zero mark. There was no wind and the stars sparkled like fire in the frosty sky. "Old Caterwaul ought to freeze tonight," thought the boy as he went in. And next morning, as he sped down the river he discovered he was right. Only the rapids at the head of Piney Reach remained open, and when he had skirted them he found himself gliding over the finest ice he had ever seen. It was a perfect sheet of transparent crystal, as clear as glass, that gave resiliently under his weight. Delighted, he cut figures on its black surface, and tested his skates in a burst of speed. Near the foot of the Reach he stopped and cut a hole in the ice with his jack-knife. It was hardly more than an inch thick, but tough enough to be safe as long as the cold weather held.

The sun was up now and its slanting beams lit up the stream-bed, so that Brad could see each golden pebble and moss-covered boulder below him. "Gee," he laughed to himself, "talk about your glass-bottomed boats! Wish that old trout from under Indian Rock would swim past here now!"

So long did he spend looking down into the sun-bright river that he barely missed being late for school. As he mounted the steps, Lin Kennedy stopped him for a second. "The boys say you're scared to race Riggs Jenkins," he said. "Listen—I'll lend you those new hockey-skates of mine—"

But Brad laughed and shook his head. "I'll use these old-timers," he replied. "Tell the gang to fix it up for this noon."

When the twelve o'clock bell rang there was a rush for the mill-pond.

"Where's the big race going to be?" someone asked.

"I don't care," said Jenkins, affecting boredom. "I

told Townsend I'd take him on, any time, any place."

Brad was putting on his skates. "All right," he called, "the slickest ice in the township is up the Caterwaul at Piney Reach. There's a half-mile straightaway, smooth as glass. We can get up there in five minutes."

A few boys wanted the test held nearer home, but the majority had no objection to missing lunch in order to be present at the event. And in a moment, twenty or thirty of them were skating jubilantly up the little river.

At the beginning of the new ice, the crowd paused to discuss the conditions of the race. "I'll tell you," said Kennedy. "The rest of you go up to the head of the Reach and draw a finish line. I'll stay here to start them, and then I'll follow along."

With whoops and cheers the spectators departed for the other end of the course. Brad knelt and tightened his skate straps, then stood by while Kennedy cut a straight line in the ice with the heel of his skate. "All right—they're about up there by now," said the volunteer starter. "Guess you can take your places."

Side by side the two boys lined up, their bodies bent tensely forward. "On your marks!" yelled Kennedy. "Get set!—Go!"

Jenkins got away before the final syllable had sounded —stealing a full stride on Brad. But the mountain boy took half a dozen running strokes that kept him at his rival's heels. Then they were off to the ringing *zip—zip—zip* of steel on ice.

Jenkins was setting a dizzy pace. He was bowed far over, hands locked behind him in true professional style. The long, gleaming blades of his racing-skates flashed with the steady rhythm of pistons. Brad, following close, sent up a silent cheer for the forgotten craftsman who had fashioned the queer contraptions strapped to his own flying feet. They were good! He could feel them answer gallantly to the powerful drive of his legs. He was holding his own.

What wind there was seemed to be blowing down-stream into their faces. Brad felt it slowing him down and cut over to the left, in the lee of the pines, where the air was still and the clear, black ice was untouched by skates. It was a wise move. He began to creep closer. Whether he was as fast as the town boy he could not tell, but he knew he had more endurance. So he stuck doggedly at it, holding his place a stride to the rear.

They were halfway up the course now. Jenkins shot a glance over his shoulder and quickened his stroke in a sudden spurt. It didn't last. After fifty yards of furious skating he dropped back once more, and Brad could hear him puffing heavily as he drew up on even terms. The farm boy knew he had him beaten. Exultantly he

THEN A STRANGE THING HAPPENED

threw more power into his stride and began to forge ahead. The crowd was in sight now, far up the Reach, yelling like mad.

"Come on, Caterwaul! Come on, Townsend! Come on, you curly-nose skates!"—they howled, for Brad was leading by a good ten yards.

Then a strange thing happened. Lin Kennedy, flying along behind the racers, saw Brad hesitate in his stroke, then whirl his body sidewise and come to a slithering stop with both skates braced to hold him. An instant later he was doubling back down the Reach, while Jenkins rushed past toward the finish line,

"What's the matter?" cried Kennedy. "Go on! Go on! You had him trimmed!"

Brad was skating slowly, staring down at the frozen surface of the river near the shore. Suddenly he checked his stride and threw himself on hands and knees, his face close to the ice. He had little breath left, but with one mittened hand he beckoned frantically to Kennedy. And when the banker's son approached, he pointed through the clear, black ice.

"Lin!" he panted. "Look! It's there—the cash-box!"

It was Kennedy's turn to be excited now. Shading his eyes he peered down into the sunlit depths of the stream and saw the corner of a metal-bound black chest protruding from under a rock, five or six feet below the surface.

"Jiminy Christmas!" the boy gasped. "That's it, sure enough! Great stuff, Brad! Let's get back to the bank and tell Father."

He rose and waved an arm to the others. "Whoopee!" he yelled. "Brad's found the money-box! They dropped it in the river!"

As the group skated back toward town, Riggs Jenkins shouldered his way to Brad's side. "I'll admit I was licked," he grinned. "And oh, boy! A thousand dollars reward! I guess you'll be able to buy all the racing-skates you want, now!"

"No," chuckled Brad, happily. "That money's spoken for. It's going to pay for an operation that'll cure Mary Sue. An' as far as the skates are concerned, I reckon I'll stick to this old pair. There must be luck in curly noses."

ANCHOR MAN

"AND WHY," asked the sweet young thing, "do they call the last runner in the relay the 'Anchor Man'?"

"Because," growled her escort, whose school had just taken a licking, "—because he generally runs as if he was anchored."

· · · · · · ·

It was about anchor men that Moose Macgregor was thinking, as he swung his six feet of brawn slowly along the turf beside the 220 straightaway. Not in the scornful terms of the old gag, however. At that particular moment he felt he would rather run anchor on the Riverdale High Relay Team than be President. He kicked a cinder moodily with his spiked toe, and turned to stroll, head down, toward the gym.

Back by the jumping pit a lean man in a sweat-shirt chewed a spear of new grass and watched him through half-closed blue eyes. Coach Carrington had handled a dozen Riverdale track teams and recognized his big captain's symptoms. Before Moose had taken a dozen strides toward the showers he heard a voice behind him.

Not loud but sharp as a pistol-crack. "Macgregor!"

He straightened up and faced about.

"Take a few starts and jog a lap in eighty seconds— no faster," said the coach. "Loosen up before you go in."

Moose nodded and went down to the chute at the end of the 220 where he would be out of the way of the distance men, loping eternally around the oval. There he dug his toe holes, took his mark, arched his back at the imaginary "Get set!", and snapped his powerful legs into a start. Over and over he did it, methodically, and after a little the scowl left his face.

There was nothing rebellious in the boy's mood. He was simply low—disgusted with himself. And the starts did him good. Seemed as if he was getting more spring into it now—a little better timing, perhaps. But he'd been practicing starts for three seasons, and he still got off like an ice-wagon.

Glancing at his wrist watch, Moose set out around the curve, at a long, slow stride that limbered his thigh muscles. Behind him he heard a thudding of feet and Dink Staples, the little, spectacled two-miler, hauled up abreast. "Pace me in, Moose," he panted. "Last lap!"

"Not on your life!" Macgregor grinned. "Eighty's my orders. And if you don't lead me home by twenty yards I'll paddle you."

Spurred by this promise, the weary Staples hoisted his spindly elbows and pounded away up the backstretch. He was waiting at the finish when Moose trotted in. There was an odd friendship between these two. They were both seniors. For three years, while the powerful Moose had been annexing letters in football, basketball and track, Dink Staples, studious, unathletic, had plugged away at his distance running. There was some endurance in his light, spare frame that carried him through where stronger boys faltered. Now at last he had made the team. He was second-string two-miler for Riverdale High.

"How'd the relay trials come out?" asked Dink, as they neared the locker-room.

"Manero out in front, eight yards or so," Moose replied. "The rest of us bunched in a blanket finish. I was third. That kid's a flash, and no mistake. The coach wouldn't tell us the time, but he admitted it wasn't worse than fifty-two."

"Gee!" breathed Dink, rapturously, "with Manero at anchor we *have* got a team this year! Ought to clean up in our division. And say—what's that Class-B High School record? Three-thirty-three and four-fifths, isn't it? Say, we might even have a chance to trim it. If three of you ran in fifty-four, and Vic Manero could turn in a fifty-one—let's see," he figured swiftly. "Yes, sir, that's a three-thirty-three mile!"

There was no answer but a muffled grunt. Moose was bent low over one of his shoes, his face turned away, and Dink looked at him with quick comprehension. Of course! Moose would be running his last relay for Riverdale. Manero was only a second-year youngster. It was too bad, in a way. And yet everybody knew Macgregor wasn't really a quarter-miler. The 880 was his distance. He could run it close to the magic two-minute mark, and his second lap was always faster than his first. That was where his strength counted—the same tough strength that made him unstoppable at fullback, and enabled him to toss the twelve-pound shot forty-four feet with no more form than a—well, than a moose!

For five minutes the scrawny Staples kept a discreet silence. But when they were rubbing down after the shower he tried to inject a word of comfort into his classmate's gloom.

"There's another trial before the race, isn't there?" he asked.

"Yeah," said Moose laconically. "Thursday."

"Maybe you'll show 'em something," remarked Dink, and started dressing with a cheerful whistle.

Time dragged slowly that week. Ordinarily the date of the University Relays came and passed without much stir in Riverdale. The school always sent a team down to the big city, backed by a handful of faithful supporters. There, year after year, they had run their legs off without glory, for there were some strong schools in their division. But this April it was different. Wherever you went in the town you heard men and boys and even girls talking about the Relays. Ever since young Victor Manero had sprinted through to take the 440 in the dual meet with Collison High, the idea of a winning relay team had tickled the fancy of the good folk of Riverdale. For the first time in history their school had four quarter-milers—four boys, at least, who could come close to averaging 54 seconds on a good track. And as the time grew shorter the buzz of excitement mounted.

Only the team itself seemed to remain calm. The boys kept strict training, worked out under the eagle eye of the coach every afternoon, and went to bed at 9:30 every night. They were in perfect condition and as playful as puppies—all, that is, except Moose Macgregor. There was a purposeful grimness about the big track captain that Coach Carrington observed with speculative interest. The final trials were held on Thursday, just two days before the race. At those trials the coach rather expected something to happen, and it did.

Dink Staples waited for his big chum that afternoon

as they left the locker-room for the field. They had had little chance for conversation during the earlier part of the week, and when opportunities did offer, Dink understood the captain's silent mood and let him alone. Now, however, he had something to say. For three days his scholarly brain had been working on an idea.

"Moose," he said, "what's the best half-mile you ever ran?"

"Two weeks ago, in the Martinsville meet," Macgregor answered, hesitating a little. "The timer's watch stopped, but I was going by my own. I caught it at 1:59, though I don't expect anybody to believe that. It was probably mighty close to two flat, though."

"Gee," murmured Dink. "And how fast was your second quarter—at a guess?"

"I don't know," Moose considered. "I came from pretty well behind, and led 'em in by ten yards or so. Must have been around fifty-six or seven."

Dink rubbed his hands with satisfaction. "Why is it," he asked cautiously, "that you get so much more speed on the second lap?"

"Oh, I just seem to get loosened up," the taller boy replied. "The old bellows feel better, and my stride is easier. Then I always have enough left for a good leg-kick in the stretch."

Staples nodded emphatically. "Just so," he said. "Now

listen, you big ox—" and he was still talking in an eager whisper as they drew near the track.

There were a few impromptu starts and the usual jogging up and down as the squad assembled.

Carrington cupped his hands. "Relay team," he called, "all over at the starting line."

It was on the other side of the field. The squad strolled across in a body, the sprinters lifting their knees in an occasional little prancing step.

Carrington looked about him. "Relay boys all here?" he asked. "Let's see—Manero—Don Schwartz—Mickey McCabe—where's the Moose? He was here a minute ago."

As if in answer there came a quick pounding of feet down the straightaway, and Macgregor dashed into the middle of the group. He had stayed behind when the others started across the field and had run up the back-stretch, around the turn, and down to meet them—not jogging, but steaming along like a fire-truck.

The coach gave him a queer look that was not wholly one of exasperation. "What in blue blazes—" he barked. "Here we are, all ready to start this trial, and now we've got to wait!"

Macgregor grinned at him, breathing deep. "Don't wait for me," he said. "I'm warmed up. Let's go!"

There was wonder in the coach's eye as he looked the

big lad up and down. But in three seconds his decision was made. "Very good," he said briskly, "it's your funeral, Moose. Take your marks—same positions as last time."

The quartet moved up to the line. Vic Manero had the pole. Next him was red-haired Mickey McCabe, then Don Schwartz, and on the outside the captain, still grinning, shuffled his spikes into the track.

"Ready?" asked the coach. "Bring your rear foot up, Manero. That's better. On your marks! Set!" And "*Bang!*" spoke his little revolver.

To Dink Staples, waiting, up on the outside of the turn, came a moment of black doubt. What if his crazy idea had done an injury to his friend? The start looked bad, but then the Moose would never be a sprint starter. Manero, the dark young Italian, was off like an arrow, his lithe legs flashing along the pole. Close at his heels ran McCabe and Schwartz, elbowing for second place. And now, cutting over to the pole behind them came the long-striding Moose. So they rounded the turn into the backstretch and Dink knew that they were all moving faster than he had ever seen them before. Manero, speeding along like the wind, had opened up four yards or so on McCabe before he reached the second turn, but Schwartz was running toe to heel with the Irish boy. And now from nowhere came a tall figure swinging big shoulders in the steady beat of his stride. And what a stride!

Dink Staples' heart came into his mouth. The Moose was passing—passing on the curve, running wide to clear the battle of his team-mates. Swiftly the little group rounded into the head of the stretch. Manero was still hugging the pole, coming down with the smooth speed of the born quarter-miler. But just outside him, and a bare five yards to the rear, pounded Macgregor.

Staples crouched, tense, gnawing at a whitened knuckle. "The old leg-drive!" he groaned to himself. "Oh, gosh! If he's still got it!" And aloud he screamed, "Moose! Come on, you Moose!"

The Moose had it. He moved faster, faster, his chin up, his big knees pumping like pistons. Manero heard him and flung a quick glance over his shoulder, then spurted like a frightened deer. They crossed the finish line with the Italian a single good stride to the fore.

The squad had been yelling like Sioux on the warpath for the last twenty seconds of that race. Now they swarmed round the runners and the coach. "Some race, Moose!" "Great work, Vic!" "Gee, but that was fast! What time did you make it, Coach?" they cried.

Carrington dropped his watch in his pocket with a grin that he couldn't conceal. "Very good time indeed," he answered. "Moose, old timer, that was the best quarter

I ever saw you run. You, too, Manero, and you, Mickey and Don. I don't mind telling you that if you all do as well day after tomorrow you'll crack the Class-B record wide open. Now we'll have some practice passing the baton, and you'll be done for the day. This trial settles your places on the team. Moose, you'll run first, and I think you'll give us a lead. McCabe and Schwartz, you'll run second and third. If you can give young Vic, here, an even start or better, he'll do the rest. All right, now we'll try passing the stick."

Moose Macgregor had gone to the showers before Staples started the last long grind of his afternoon's work. But the big half-miler was waiting, dressed, by the door when his friend came panting in. His long, freckled face was wreathed in a grin.

"Well, old porpoise," he chuckled, "your hunch was good. It wasn't your fault it didn't work. The kid's just too fast for me. But, boy, I gave him a race, didn't I?"

"Did you!" gasped Dink. "Another ten yards an' you'd have caught him sure!"

But Moose shook his head. "No," he said, "I was running all I knew. Do you know what the time was for that quarter? Fifty-one seconds! Think that over. Vic Manero's anchor, and I'll say he rates it. All I want now is for this outfit to win."

o   o   •   •   •   o   o

It rained all day Friday, in a steady, gentle drizzle. The people of Riverdale frowned at the weather from behind their windows and talked dismally, not of the benefit to their lawns and gardens, but of a slow track, and the fading chances of record time in the Relays. But when Saturday dawned the rain had ceased. A gray sky hung over the countryside and the light wind blew sharply cold. Down at the railroad station a crowd was gathering, for the town had chartered a special train for this day of days. At eight o'clock the team appeared, top-coated, and entered their car, to an accompaniment of friendly cheers. With them came Old Tom, the negro rubber, with two suitcases filled with track clothes, and shortly after, Carrington arrived.

"Well, boys," he smiled as he settled into his seat, "I had University Field on the 'phone this morning. The ground-keeper says the track's perfect. Settled by the rain and rolled for an hour before breakfast. If the grammar schools don't cut it up too much before we come on deck, it'll be the fastest track you ever ran on. Stick together when we get to town. I've got a buddy at the Alpha Delt house and we can loaf there till dressing-time. Our race is scheduled for 2:15 and we're to be ready in the locker-house at 1:30. Believe me, that means on the dot, too. They run these Relays like the

Broadway Limited—never more than a minute or two off schedule."

The hours dragged. A little after one, when they had played all the jazz records the fraternity afforded and read every jest in the three dilapidated copies of *Life*, the Riverdale team started across the campus. Pushed along with the hurrying crowd, they could not have missed their way if they had wanted. And in addition to Carrington and the old rubber, Moose Macgregor, at least, had been there before. He remembered the clammy feeling of other Relay days and gave Vic Manero a sympathetic clap on the back. He knew just how uncomfortable the scant lunch of tea and toast must feel under the Sophomore's belt. "Never mind, kid," he said. "It'll be over in another hour, and then we'll buy you the biggest platter of spaghetti in town!"

"I don't feel so hungry, Moose," the boy replied with a wan attempt at a smile. "Kind of nervous, I guess."

A thousand youngsters swarmed in the big gymnasium. They were everywhere—dressing and undressing—boys of all sizes and ages from fifth grade to college. They wore every conceivable costume. There were ragged little chaps in over-size jerseys and flapping sneakers. There were tall, well-mannered prep school boys in expensive-looking track shoes and immaculate school colors. You could tell which ones were waiting and which had already run. One group was silent, pale and fidgety. The other, hilarious with released energy. Here and there a boy lay in a corner sick with nervousness or with the strain of his race. And every five minutes a red-faced man with a megaphone entered and called the teams for the next event.

The Riverdale boys got into their suits, under Coach Carrington's hawk-like scrutiny. He examined every ankle-brace and tested the lacing of every shoe. Then one by one they stretched on a bench and submitted to the strong, soothing hands of Old Tom. Deftly he massaged their leg muscles, loosening the sinews of their calves, kneading his oily black knuckles into the flesh of their thighs, front and back. "Goin' to run, dis day," he crooned as he worked. "Goin' to show yo' heels to all dese yer other trash. Goin' to pull me out ma fo' bucks, what ah done laid on yo' all."

Two o'clock passed and two-five, while they sat in an uneasy row. On the tick of two-ten the man with the megaphone gave them their call. "Up-state high schools, Class B," he bawled. "Collison, Greenfield, Jonesport, Riverdale, Martinsville, Braxton."

"And points north," muttered Moose Macgregor, for it sounded for all the world like a train announcement. He strode out in the lead, pushing the small fry out of his path. The hard, gray light of day made him blink as he came through the gate onto the field. And there was a chill in the fitful breeze.

Huddled in their sweaters, the little knot of Riverdale runners felt suddenly insignificant in the teeming bowl of the stadium. A race was just finishing and forty thousand spectators were yelling encouragement to the leaders, Hardly had the last straggler crossed the line when busy officials were calling the starters for the next race to take their places. With machine-like precision the winners and the time were flashed on the huge score-board and announced over the public address system. And ten seconds later the gun sent another race on its way.

Shivering with nervousness the Riverdale boys watched the runners fight for the pole on the first turn. Then Carrington called them to him. He spoke with an easy smile that belied the tenseness of his own nerves. "Just take this like any other race," he said. "The only thing that can beat you is yourselves. Keep your heads. Don't let anybody run you out in the backstretch. Hold your own stride and have something left for the sprint but not too much. Whatever else you do, pass that baton clean and sure. Now, Moose," he grinned, "better loosen up those legs on the turf."

The captain needed no urging. He sprinted fifty yards up the inside of the oval and back, then did it again.

When he returned to the little knot of Riverdalers, the coach felt of his legs. "Just right," he nodded. "Keep moving a little. Don't cool off. The rest of you might limber up a bit now."

Moose looked around at the other teams ready for his race. Many of the men he had seen before. Bill March of Braxton had beaten him in a dual-meet quarter the year before. He was running anchor of course. Tommy Holman of Collison was a good egg—a consistent 53-second man. And there were others whose names he couldn't remember, but whose faces, distorted with effort, he had watched in fighting finishes on up-state tracks. His nervousness left him suddenly and he felt steady and strong. He peeled off his sweater and someone pinned a team-number to the back of his jersey. The last circuit of the other race had started.

An assistant starter called the first-lap runners to the side of the track. Into the hand of each he put a baton—a light stick of wood something over an inch in diameter and about a foot in length. Moose tested its weight in his strong grip, made sure it was dry and would not slip out of his hand, for he had seen such things happen.

There were six teams entered in the race. Collison High had the pole and Moose was in number four position, third from the outside. As far as he was concerned it was as good a place as any other. He knew his limitations as a starter. They were lining up now. Through the haze of sound Moose heard a shrill yell somewhere in the stand above him—"Do your stuff, Moose—you long-legged son-of-a-gun!" Good old Dink, up there pulling for him! He waved the baton and took his toe holes.

Moose knew the gray-haired starter and his ways. He was a fast worker. Here it came.

"On your marks . . . get set" . . . *bang!*

With the gun he was off and in the first ten strides he found himself in third place on the pole. The Jonesport boy at his left had been caught flat-footed by the quickness of the start. Moose sped around the first curve holding his position at the heels of the Greenfield runner, while Tommy Holman set the pace. But when they were two-thirds of the way around the turn his eye caught a sudden dark flash on his right. It was the colored boy from Martinsville High, running as if possessed. He had come from outside, sprinting wide on the curve, and before any of the leaders knew it he had shot past them into the first straightaway.

The sight was too much for the Greenfield lad. He quickened his stride and dashed out past Holman, giving chase to the black phantom. The temptation was in Moose's muscles, too, but he held himself in and simply

"ON YOUR MARKS . . . GET SET" . . . BANG!

closed up the gap between himself and the steady Collison runner. He had raced against these impetuous chaps before. And he had never seen one win.

Up the backstretch they went with no change of place. Moose was going fast and smooth. And as they neared the second turn he could see the tired negro dropping back. He was only twenty yards ahead now. Moose grinned inwardly. "Pulled his cork!" he muttered. The Greenfield boy, driven still by his urge to run in front, fought his way around the darky on the curve and took the lead. Moose could see the high, uncertain action of his knees and the outstretched neck that meant disaster. But the youngster was game. He was still half a dozen strides in front at the head of the final stretch.

Someone challenged on Moose's right as they broke out of the turn, and the Riverdale captain shook out his long legs in a quicker stride. Holman was putting on steam, too. There it lay—a hundred yards of broad, straight cinder-path ahead of them—and at the end a line of second men strung across the track. They jumped and beckoned. Mickey McCabe's red head, fourth from the pole! Like a homing pigeon Moose drove for that flaming torch of hair.

Elbow to elbow, he and Holman came down the stretch. They shot past the colored lad, past the staggering Greenfield runner. Only thirty yards to go—now twenty. Little by little, Moose pulled ahead, sprinting fiercely. He had him! With a quick snap of the arm he laid the baton squarely in Mickey's palm, and for a second or two he ran beside him stride for stride. Then, panting, he came off the track. He had given the little Irishman a four-yard lead.

Carrington met him with a happy grin. "Great quarter, old boy!" he said. "Here's your sweater. Get into it."

Don Schwartz had already gone to the starting line, but Vic Manero was waiting for him, eyes wide with admiration. "Gee, Moose," he sputtered, "if—if I can run that way!" It was the sincerest kind of compliment. Moose grabbed him by his arms. "Run *that* way!" he snorted. "You'll make me look like a cart-horse! Why, you're going to break that record, boy! Say, watch old Mickey go!"

The carrot-topped sprinter was flying up the far side of the track, still holding his lead at the turn. A lanky runner with the figure 6 of Braxton High fluttering on his shoulders pushed up abreast of the Collison man and fought him for second place all the way around the curve.

"He's done!" cried Moose. "He worked too hard for that."

But Carrington didn't agree with him. "No," he said,

"I've watched that boy before. He's strong." And so it proved, for the Braxton sprinter was close to McCabe's shoulder as they came tearing down the straightaway.

The little red-head's face was a twisted mask of agony. He was running on his heart now and nothing else. But he stuck, to the end, and sent Don Schwartz away a stride in front. Then he came staggering across the track, blind and sick.

Vic Manero darted past Macgregor to catch his tottering team-mate. And as Mickey stumbled into his arms the sharp steel of his spikes came down on the Italian's instep. The disaster fell so swiftly that Moose's brain was numb. He stood there holding the two of them in his big arms and looked blankly into the white face of the coach.

"Number four—Riverdale—where's your last man?" barked a voice from the track, and Moose snapped out of his daze. "Here, Coach," he said, "take care of 'em. I'll run—it's all we can do, now."

"Wait—let me think!" Carrington was staring at a forlorn hope. "The rules say, 'If a runner is for any reason unable to start, his place may be taken by any properly qualified substitute who is a student of the same school.' Nothing in that to stop you. But, Moose, it's no good. You'd never get halfway 'round!"

Moose already had his sweater off. "Well," he grinned,

"I'm warmed up, anyhow." And he walked to the line. The pack was already rounding into the last straightaway, and the anchor men were eager to be off.

Dink Staples, high up in the stand above the starting line, rubbed furiously at his spectacles, then whipped them back on his nose. His eyesight had not played him a trick. Down in that row of crazy jumping-jacks stood a big figure, oddly quiet. Dink had not noticed the accident to Manero. He had been following Don Schwartz's gallant race. And at the sight of Moose Macgregor in the line he nearly fell over on the man in front of him. Then he caught sight of the Italian, limping toward the locker-house on the coach's shoulder, and realized what had happened. "Moose!" he gurgled, but the roar of the crowd drowned him out. And at that instant the tide of runners surged past. The last lap had started.

In the long seconds that the Moose spent on the starting-line he had felt an odd sense of triumph. He was running his last relay for Riverdale all right—running it with a vengeance! Funny he didn't feel tired, though. Not yet. He saw Don Schwartz's tortured face battling toward him down the stretch. A game guy, Don! He was in front, too, by thunder!

He took two strides and the baton was in his outstretched hand. Then he was shooting diagonally across the track to the pole. In his memory with comic distinctness clung the fleeting glimpse he had had of Schwartz's mouth, open and bewildered at the sight of him.

That was all he thought about as he pounded around the turn. Then it came to him with chilling suddenness that he had been taking it too fast. His knee action didn't seem to be so smooth, and there was a deadness about his flying feet. How close were the others? He wouldn't look back, but his ears were strained for the crunch of cinders. The sound came, halfway up the backstretch. Out of the corner of his right eye he could see hands pumping. Someone was passing him. Well, let 'em. His instinct told him it was too soon.

The other runner was three strides ahead before he cut in. No one tried to jostle Moose. His size was a warning. He saw the big "6" on the jersey—Braxton. It must be his old enemy, Bill March.

Moose steadied his stride and kept pace with the new leader. Another sound of feet on the curve and a flushed face crept level with his, only to drop back, spent with effort, after a dozen steps. That finished the pack, he thought. It was between him and March, now—Riverdale and Braxton. With an odd feeling of detachment he wondered about his legs. Was the drive still there? They were well into the last straightaway, but he wouldn't try it yet. His feet were too dead to be sure.

Forty yards to the finish now, and his rival still a stride or two in the lead. Moose was numb all over. No, there was no kick left. And what of it?

Then a high-pitched yell pierced his tired brain. "Moose! Come on you *anchor man!*" Dink Staples had found his voice at last.

Something clicked in the big runner's mind and lifted his laboring knees. To his surprise he found March right beside him now. Wabbling! The Braxton boy was done. And there before his hazy eyes was a wavering line of white. With a last burst of effort, Moose flung his wracked body at the tape, and fell a yard beyond it to slide cruelly along the cinders.

.　　.　　.　　.　　.　　.　　.

Down in the locker-house, half an hour later, a howling dervish in spectacles burst in on the comparative peace of the Riverdale Relay squad.

"Looks like a hospital," Dink observed gaily, when he had hugged the team individually and collectively. "Mickey'll feel better when he's surrounded a steak. And Vic, your foot will be well in plenty of time to win a couple more relays for Riverdale. As for you, Moose, those honorable scars on your face and arms will fittingly commemorate this great occasion. And speaking of keepsakes—" he pulled a folded newspaper from his pocket— "here's one you'll want to frame." As one man the squad leaned over Moose's shoulder and read. It was in the "late news" column of the Night Extra, just off the press:

CLASS-B HIGH SCHOOL RECORD SMASHED

RIVERDALE WINS THRILLING RACE

TO SET NEW TIME OF 3:32⅖

The mile relay record for Class-B High Schools which has stood for eight years was broken today by a strong team from Riverdale High, which beat Braxton in a brutal finish, setting a new mark of 3:32⅖. The race was featured by the running of the Macgregor twins. "Moose" Macgregor, the better known of the duo, ran first and turned in a quarter in 51 seconds flat. His brother, running anchor, could do no better than 53, but his game fight down the stretch to win brought the crowd to its feet with one of the greatest thrills of this year's Relay Games.

"Coach," said Dink solemnly, lifting the bandaged Moose to his feet, "may I present the twins!"

F*UNNY* how you can go through four years of college with a man—see him every day—form an apparently bomb-proof estimate of his character—and then have all your ideas blown to bits in one flash of action.

I thought I knew all about Red Lassiter, until an afternoon in June of our last year at State. . . .

But to give you the picture, I'm going back to a day in February of that year, and the first call for baseball practice.

Down on the bulletin board in the Athletic Association office, a big sheet of paper had been posted that morning. "Baseball candidates please sign below," it was headed, and already nearly sixty names had been scribbled on it.

As sports editor of the *Daily* I needed that list for the next day's paper, so I stopped on my way from an afternoon Lab period. Beefy Gilman's massive back completely hid the paper from my view. He was standing there so absorbed in the list that he didn't notice my approach. Laboriously he wrote his name with a stub of pencil under the heading, "Catcher." Then he scanned the sheet again, his round, cherubic face as wistful as a hungry little boy's in front of a bakery window.

I gave him an affectionate crack over the head with a two-pound note-book. "How's prospects this spring, Beef?" I asked.

His smile would have fooled anybody who didn't know him as well as I did. "Oh, so-so," he piped. He had a little, high voice that always sounded comical coming from that vast body. "The general run of catchers don't look so hot. Maybe this is my year. Let's see—there's—"

He was interrupted by the appearance of a newcomer —a well-set, husky chap with careless auburn hair— who pushed between us without apology and drew a big gold pen from his pocket. At the foot of the catcher's list he signed with a firm hand—"Raymond J. Lassiter." There was confidence in that signature—and finality. The long cross on the "t" was as straight and sure as his throw to second. He gave us an impersonal nod and strode away.

Beefy's eyes followed him, full of honest admiration. Then he turned back to me with a sheepish grin.

"I was starting to say," he stammered, "that Wolf and Hunter and Goodrich are fair catchers but not world-beaters. Then there are a couple of Sophs that

I don't know much about. That leaves me—and Lassiter."

The pause after that name was eloquent. He knew, and I knew, that he might just as well have said "me—and Mickey Cochrane." Red Lassiter had been our first-string catcher ever since he came up from the Freshman nine. No doubt about it—he was one of the best athletes we ever had at State. A sensational football halfback, and a star forward on the basketball team. But it was on the diamond that he shone brightest.

Even a mask and pads couldn't disguise the sure grace of that lad in motion. Whatever happened he was in the play, doing the right thing, and you couldn't help watching him. He was fearless at the plate. He could hold the smokiest fast ball of our wildest southpaw. And he was such a consistent hitter that he always batted third instead of down at the tail of the order, where catchers are supposed to belong. To top it off, his family was one of the wealthiest and most prominent in our part of the country. Naturally his name appeared often in the big city papers. He was applepie for the sports reporters.

All this hadn't helped Red's popularity at college. Rightly or wrongly he was regarded as "high-hat" and a publicity seeker. But while he never could have been elected captain, everybody knew he was the real mainspring of our ball-team. When he was in there we won games.

Beefy heaved a gusty sigh. "Gee," he said, "I'd sure like to have my letter to show for these four years."

"Don't worry, kid," I laughed. "You'll make 'em all step, this spring. You're looking great. Lost some weight, haven't you?"

I knew that would cheer him up.

"Yes, sir," he said, brightening. "I've been working on the rowing machines all winter. Got off about seven pounds."

"Hmm," I remarked with due seriousness. "Seven pounds—that brings you down to a mere two hundred and ninety-odd, doesn't it? Well, good luck, Gil. I'll see you at supper."

I was a fraternity brother of Gilman's and had known him for the best part of four college years. His undiscouraged effort to be a Varsity catcher had become a tradition at State. He was the hardest-working boy on the squad, and the best-liked. For three seasons he hadn't missed a day's practice. Every year hoping for his letter—and still able to grin when June rolled around and he was left out. Poor old Beefy!

We had a good ball-team that spring. It was my job on the *Daily* to follow them pretty closely and I not only scored all the games but dropped in regularly at practice to see if I could wangle enough news out of the coach to make a story. There were twenty games on the schedule and now we were down to the final contest with only two defeats chalked up against us. Beefy Gilman had had his turn with the other catchers in some of the minor engagements. But in all the big games it was Lassiter who worked behind the bat.

The Sheldon game has always been our letter-game at State. It's that way in every sport, right through the year. You can't wear one of those big Varsity letters unless you've been in at least part of a contest with Sheldon. The two schools are only fifty miles apart, and have about the same number of students. And spirit— oh, boy—until you've seen the ninth inning of a tight game between Sheldon and State you don't know how hard colleges can take their baseball.

The afternoon before that last fateful game, I sat as usual on the bench beside Coach Bill Ginty. He had finished knocking out grounders and was watching his pitchers practice. The only noise on the field was the steady thud—thud—thud of horsehide in the big mitts, and the chat of the catchers as they tossed back balls to the moundsmen. That was one of the things Ginty insisted on—a constant stream of encouragement from behind the plate. He picked catchers as Rockne used to pick quarterbacks, for a loud voice and a cocky air. And there was no doubt it helped the morale of his teams.

"Well," I asked, "any casualties to report, Coach?"

The old big-leaguer shook his head. His eye was on Red Lassiter and he was frowning. "Look at him!" he growled. "Grandest backstop prospect I ever coached, and because his dad's got so much money, the boy'll never see the inside of a pro uniform."

"No," I agreed, "probably not. But look at what he's done in college. You've got that to be proud of."

I fished an afternoon paper out of my pocket. One of the city reporters had been out to the campus the day before with a camera.

"Here," I said, opening up the sports page. "Read the story about your first-string catcher!"

Under a striking action picture was a two-column head:

STATE STAR ROUNDS OUT
GREAT RECORD TOMORROW

"RED" LASSITER HAS CHANCE TO REACH 300-INNING
MARK IN CATCHING LAST GAME OF CAREER

When Raymond J. "Red" Lassiter dons pad and mask tomorrow afternoon he will be on the way to hanging up a record untouched in the annals of State athletics. As ranking Varsity catcher for the past three years, this versatile athlete has caught every inning of every major game on the schedule. A glance at official score-sheets for this three-year period shows that he has played through 31 games, including the memorable 13-inning Sheldon contest of last year, and has caught a total of 291 innings.

Tomorrow's final game with Sheldon will be Lassiter's last in a State uniform. Nothing short of a tornado or an earthquake can keep him from adding another nine innings to his total and bringing it up to an even 300—a mark that is not likely to be broken. "Red" has a lot of pride in the fact that he has never been taken out of a game in his whole college career. And he'll be in there tomorrow working as never before.

"Huh!" grunted the coach, and thrust the paper back into my hand. His eye went back to the battery practice but it was not at Lassiter that he looked, nor at the pitchers. I followed his glance and found it fixed on Beefy Gilman.

Beefy was easy to find. In the middle of the line of receivers his bulk loomed like a mountain. There he squatted, slapping the ball into his mitt—three hundred pounds of perspiring earnestness and everlasting good nature.

"Talk about records," I couldn't help thinking, "there's a boy that must have warmed up ten thousand fidgety fingers, and panted after a million wide balls!"

I started to speak what was in my mind, but the grim look on Ginty's face checked me. Instead I pulled out my notebook and pencil. "Any news on the line-up for tomorrow?" I asked in my best reportorial manner. "Who's likely to be your starting pitcher?"

The coach turned on me with a glare. "Young man," he said, "you ought to know by this time that I pick my batteries the day o' the game. Either Jones or Sullivan'll pitch, and you'll have to make the best story you can out o' that. No change in the batting order."

He rose abruptly and I knew it was my cue to leave. However, I waited in the locker-room till the squad came off the field. There were still two hours before the paper went to press, and most of my copy was in.

In a few minutes Gilman emerged from the showers, swabbing his vast back with a towel that looked entirely inadequate.

"Hi, Bo!" he squeaked at me. "Two shakes an' I'll go home with you."

He was almost as good as his word. For a human elephant, he could move around surprisingly fast. When we were out under the trees, Beefy gave me one of his infectious grins. "Wow, but it was hot on that field!" he chuckled. "Bet I lost another pound. If baseball lasted all year 'round I'd have a figure like a Hollywood bathing girl. Let's get a quart of ice cream before supper."

"Brother Gilman," I replied austerely, "you know that training rules prohibit the consumption of food between meals. Also the house steward is even now placing our frugal repast on the table."

"Yeah," he sighed. "I forgot I was still in training. Well, tomorrow it'll be all over—for keeps."

We joined a group of the brothers who were lolling on the house steps. And hardly had we found comfortable spots of our own when Red Lassiter walked past in the direction of his own fraternity—a rich and exclusive one on the upper circle. He gave us a short nod and a cool "Hello, boys," and went on. There was a certain arrogance in his easy stride.

The gang on the steps kept silence till he was out of ear-shot. Then Ike Jolley spoke up in a tone of affected boredom.

"Dear me, yes," he said. "Mr. Raymond J. 'three-hundred-inning' Lassiter, the well-known backstop and cotillion-leader. Did any of you see the blurb in the *Herald* this afternoon?"

It appeared that everybody had except Beefy Gilmàn, and I loaned him my paper—somewhat against my will. The supper call came just then and I ambled inside with the crowd. But Beefy stayed, reading every word of the Lassiter article.

When he came in his broad face was beaming with honest delight. "Gee, that's swell!" he cried. "Three hundred innings! An' where'd we be without Lassiter to catch? It means a lot just to know a guy like that and sit on the same bench with him!"

"Yep," said I, a bit grudgingly. "No doubt about it —he's the best catcher we ever had at State. And now, Falstaff, it's time to eat—do you hear—*eat!*"

.   .   .   .

That Saturday of the Sheldon game was one of the loveliest of an unusually lovely spring. By two-thirty, when I took my place at the scorer's table, the stands were already well-filled. A lot of people always come up from the city to our big games, and today the crowd was larger than usual. Back of the Sheldon bench there was a cheering section of their undergraduates nearly 2,000 strong. And of course every State student who could hobble to the field was on hand.

The Sheldon squad occupied the diamond for the moment, and the snappy way they flipped the ball around made me nervous. They had a fast, aggressive team, and I knew they would be battling all the way.

Over back of third, three of our pitchers were warming up—Whiff Jones, the long, lean right-hander with his easy side-arm motion—Lefty Sullivan, slipping them in fast—and Johnny Ray, a sturdy young Sophomore who had shown up well in several minor games. I could see Bill Ginty watching every ball thrown, out of the corner of his eye.

Game time was drawing close. The band struck up "Forward, State," the Sheldon nine ran off the field, and one of the umpires came over to our bench to get Ginty's battery selections. I looked down there and got a lump in my throat. Beefy Gilman was kneeling in the dirt in front of Red Lassiter, buckling the shin-guards around his idol's legs.

The blue-coated official stalked back to the plate and raised his arm for silence. "Batteries for the game," he bellowed. "For Sheldon, Winters and Gage. For State, Sullivan and Lassiter."

There was loud applause from the stands. Then, to the accompaniment of a State "Long Yell," our team trotted out to take their positions. A good-looking outfit in their spick-and-span white uniforms. Quickly I checked the players against the names on the score-sheet before me. Captain Joe Dove at short, Bert Kane and Tom Denby on first and second, little Mike Kelly on third. The regular fly-chasers—Deuce Diamond, Andy Schultz and Rube Richards—holding down the outfield.

Lefty Sullivan took the new ball and tossed over his practice shots. He was a tall, strongly-built boy with a world of speed—practically unbeatable on his good days.

Sheldon's famous "Rip-em-up" cheer echoed across the horseshoe, and their lead-off man stepped up to the plate with a belligerent tug at his cap. The game was on.

Lefty got his signal and nodded. Then he broke out of his usual jerky wind-up with a fast ball that went higher and higher, till Lassiter's lifted mitt barely touched it. Happy jeers arose from the Sheldon section. I don't pretend to have mysterious powers of clairvoyance, but right then I could have prophesied that Sullivan was due for an early shower.

He fidgeted with the next one and grooved it over the plate. The batter, who had settled down confidently to wait for a walk, took the stick off his shoulder a split second too late and missed. It was State's turn to cheer. Lefty took the ball and tried to slip over a "sleeper," but his quick pitch was wide and low. Instead of taking his time and steadying down, the big southpaw threw hurriedly again—third ball.

Through the shouts from the Sheldon stand, Red Lassiter's voice cut clear and confident: "All right, old kid, this one'll fool him. Put it right here." But with the sock of the ball in the mitt, the Sheldon man tossed away his bat and trotted down to first.

Lassiter went halfway to the mound talking to Lefty. And the next ball pitched was hit for a screaming single just over the first-baseman's head. Runners on third and first and Sheldon's big guns coming up. This time our captain ran in from short to slap the big Irishman on the back. It was no good. Lefty looked glum as he wound up. He threw a couple that acted as if they were going to nick the corner, but the umpire called them both wide. And then the worst happened. The husky at the plate saw a fast one coming over the middle and hoisted it into the lap of a co-ed, somewhere behind left field.

While the rooters across the diamond hooted and howled with glee, the whole State infield came in and joined the conclave around the box. If ever a pitcher had moral support, Lefty had, but it was too late to steady him now.

The fourth man up was Sheldon's captain and first-sacker, a smart ball-player named Powers. He stood there grinning and took his base on five pitched balls. Sullivan didn't wait for any more. He flung his glove down and went toward the bench, looking blackly at the ground.

Bill Ginty was motioning to Jones, who had stayed in the bull-pen tossing easy ones to Beefy Gilman. The lanky righthander went to the mound, accompanied by Red Lassiter. I saw the catcher glance toward Powers, where he stood jauntily on first, and I could guess what he was saying. The Sheldon captain had the reputation of being the fanciest base-stealer in college baseball.

If Sullivan had acted nervous when he took the hill,

there were no such signs on Whiff Jones' part. He was a farmer from back in the hills, drawling, deliberate, cool as a cucumber. An ideal relief pitcher. He lacked something of Lefty's speed, but he had a good cross-fire and a slow-breaking curve that was hard for sluggers to handle.

Jones finished his warm-up and toed the slab. I couldn't see Red's signal, but I had a hunch it would be for a low one, outside. Powers had taken a long lead off first. As the pitch started, three things happened at once. The Sheldon captain sprinted down the base-path. The batter lunged in an unsuccessful effort to bunt. And Red Lassiter skipped a pace to the right, snaring the wide ball close to the ground. Without standing up he rifled it down to the waiting glove of Tom Denby on second. The runner was out by a foot.

A frenzied roar greeted this piece of strategy, and the way the ball flew around the infield gave evidence of renewed morale.

There was one strike on the man at the plate, and before the cheering died down Whiff had thrown two more across—both broad curves that broke just out of reach.

The next man up popped futilely to Kane, on first, and the visitors' half of the inning was over.

Those three runs on the scoreboard looked like a

pretty big lead, right at the start, but our team set out manfully to whittle it down. It wasn't an easy assignment. Facing us was Frosty Winters, a fast-ball pitcher with a great college record. He had been scouted by three major league clubs, and rumor had it that he would join the Yankees as soon as he had his diploma. We had been trying for three seasons to knock him out of the box, and had never succeeded.

Joe Dove led off our batting order and was out on a close decision at first. Deuce Diamond fanned on a called third strike. Red Lassiter cracked one past the third-baseman and stretched it to a double on a poor throw-in. Then big Andy Schultz, the heavy-shouldered Dutchman who patrolled left field for State, brought his long bat to the plate. Winters knew how to pitch to him and fooled him with two that were low and inside. But he must have been a little careless on the next one, for Andy lashed a hard-hit Texas-leaguer over short. Red Lassiter was coming fast. He rounded third going like the wind, and the coacher sent him on. It was crazy baseball but the team was in a mood to take chances. Red sailed into the plate feet-first in a cloud of dust, at the instant when the catcher took the throw. The umpire's voice couldn't be heard above the tumult, but he stretched his hands, palms down. We had a run.

As it turned out the gamble was justified, for a

moment later Bert Kane flied to third and our rally was over.

The game tightened up in the second. Whiff Jones was pitching cagily and the fielders were on their toes. An easy grounder, another strike-out and a long fly into Rube Richards' hands kept Sheldon off the bases.

In our half Mike Kelly got on, by dint of a scratchy single, but Richards and Denby failed to advance him. And Whiff Jones, true to his nick-name, fanned for the last out.

The third inning went by, and the fourth, and not a man on either side got as far as the keystone sack.

It began to look like a pitchers' battle. Encouraged by Lassiter's steady chatter, old Jonesy continued to throw them with amazing cunning. Again in the fifth, he set three Sheldon men down in succession, and the top of our order came to bat. Joe Dove had fire in his eye, but it didn't prevent his taking a cool look at three of Winters' shoots that weren't quite close enough. Two whizzing strikes came over. Then the sixth ball missed the edge of the plate and Joe took first.

Deuce Diamond waited while a strike and a ball went by, and guessed correctly that the next one would be across. He choked his bat and dribbled a bunt down the third-base line for a perfect sacrifice.

The State crowd, which had been sitting tense and

silent, was aroused by now, and the hand Red Lassiter got as he came to the plate would have done honor to the Bambino himself. I could hear him riding the rival catcher while he dug his spikes in. The Sheldon backstop must have been a bit flustered, for he had to try three times before Winters would accept his signal. The embryo big-leaguer scowled each time he shook his head, and his wrath was mounting visibly.

It was no surprise to me—and certainly none to Lassiter—when the ball came smoking straight over with vicious speed. Red was ready. No time for a full swing, but he took a quick cut at it and connected. With the crack of the bat he was off. The spectators surged to their feet, watching the ball sail up and out.

In the famous State horseshoe there is no stand back of center—nothing to stop a rolling ball but its own loss of momentum. Lassiter's hit had taken the centerfielder by surprise. He made a desperate backward leap, but the ball grazed his fingertips and bounded on. Red flashed across second at the same moment that Joe Dove jogged over the plate. He never turned his head but ran for third, pulled onward by Tom Denby's frantic gestures from the coacher's box. Far out in the green spaces the Sheldon fielder came up with the ball and relayed the throw to short. But Red was still traveling. No need for a slide this time. He crossed the rubber standing up, and I entered the tying run on the score-sheet.

The bellowing horde in the State stand had been treated to one of the biggest thrills in baseball—a fielded home-run—and there was no curbing their enthusiasm. When the uproar had subsided a little, the head cheer-leader called something through his megaphone. The massed students came back strong with a yell for Lassiter, and then—all in unison—"Two—hundred—and ninety-six innings!" they chanted.

Red, on his way back to the bench, flushed clear to the roots of his carroty hair at those words. He didn't strut or wave to the crowd as another hero might have done. He simply looked confused and uncomfortable. As quickly as possible he slipped into his place and began strapping on his leg-armor.

Back on the diamond, Frosty Winters had cooled off and was bearing down again. He tricked Schultz with a change of pace and flashed a third strike past him. And Kane hit a low fly that was grabbed at short.

With the score tied, going into the sixth, Jones looked unbeatable. His wind-up was as deliberate as ever, but he was putting all he had on every ball he pitched. One after another, the Sheldon batters came up and either fanned or popped out.

The State nine, on the other hand, had tasted blood

and wanted more. In our half of the inning Mike Kelly swaggered up to the plate like a fighting-cock and slashed out a two-bagger. Rube Richards moved him to third with a sacrifice fly. Denby walked. It began to appear that the great Frosty Winters was softening up.

Whiff Jones chose this occasion for one of his rare hits—a beautiful three-base wallop that brought in Kelly and Denby. And sure enough, Winters departed.

The new pitcher was a rosy-cheeked youngster who looked easy. He let another hit from Joe Dove's bat drive in Jones before he wound up the inning by striking out Deuce Diamond. That gave us a three-run lead, and the game certainly looked as if it was on ice.

In the first half of the seventh, it still looked that way. Jones passed a man, and was hit for a fluky single. But he went on, imperturbable as ever, and pitched himself out of the hole. The next batter slapped a grounder into Denby's hands for a double play. And the final out came when one of Sheldon's heaviest hitters knocked a sky-high foul back of the first-base line. It was nearer first than home, but Red Lassiter had his mask off and was sprinting in pursuit before the echo of the blow had died away.

"Mine!" he yelled, waving Bert Kane back. Straight for the enemy bench he sped and dove over the scattering players to come up with the ball in his hand—

as hair-raising a catch as was ever seen in any stadium.

Close behind me in the State section I heard a student growl the word "Grandstander!" But his voice was drowned instantly in a tidal wave of cheering. "Lassiter—Lassiter—Lassiter," chanted the State crowd, "—two—hundred—and ninety-eight innings!"

I was standing up, like everybody else, and I could see Red Lassiter plainly, in spite of the distance. His flushed face wore a queer, tight-mouthed look. And suddenly he sat down on the visitors' bench, leaning forward and feeling of his ankle. Kane and Jones broke through the knot of Sheldon players that had gathered around the catcher. They helped him to his feet once more, but when he tried to take a step he shook his head. Apparently it was his ankle that was hurt. Hopping on one foot and leaning on his team-mate's shoulders, Red was brought back to his own side of the field.

Hurriedly I left the scoring-table and rushed down to join the group around the injured star. His shoe was off when I arrived, and the trainer was starting to work with a roll of bandage. Red leaned over toward the coach, saying something in a voice too low for the rest of us to hear. Ginty's lips were grim, inscrutable. At last he gave a nod and stood up.

"Gilman!" he barked. "You're batting for Lassiter. Get along out there!"

Beefy staggered as if he had been hit. "B-b-but—" he was beginning, when the coach cut him short.

"Do you hear?" he snapped. "Go on out to the plate!" And almost violently he pushed Beefy in the direction of the bat-pile.

I'll never forget that heavyweight's expression, as he ambled out on the field. Dazed—incredulous—shining-eyed—like a kid who has seen Santa Claus. And the crowd! First there was a stunned silence. Then they were up, cheering like mad—Sheldon rooters as well as our own—for Beefy's mammoth figure had been a bull-pen spectacle through three years of diamond conflicts.

There was some good-natured horsing from the Sheldon side, but he stood up there and took it with a grin. After the first two had gone by for a ball and a strike, he braced his thick arms and pumped a solid single to center. It might have been the start of another big inning, but Sheldon's youthful pitcher had different ideas. He mowed our sluggers down in order, and the session ended with the fat boy hopefully hugging first.

Beefy still wore that ecstatic look as he struggled into his pads and came puffing out to catch the eighth—his first inning in a big game. He took a couple of practice throws from the grinning Whiff Jones. Then he crouched behind the plate and pounded his fist in the mitt. "Okay, Jonesy, ol' boy!" he yelled. "He's just another one. Put him in his place!"

Even the batter laughed when Gilman's high voice cracked in a squeak of excitement, but that comic relief was just what the team needed. It broke the strain and brought a gleeful chorus of encouragement from all around the infield. "Attaboy, Beef! We're with you! Let's go!"

And Jones cut the corner with a beautiful strike. He was pitching as I had never seen him pitch before—bearing down with deceptive speed and mixing in those wide, slow curves of his. The visitors were a grim crew now. They wanted this game, and there had to be some hitting if they were to pull it out of the fire. When they swung it was with vicious force. The first man struck at two without connecting, then pounded a foul fly off third that Kelly gobbled up. The second batter was fooled by a couple of benders, but he found the next one with a powerhouse swing and sent it on a screaming line to right field. Only a marvelous shoestring catch by Richards averted a sure two-bagger.

With two down, and two strikes on the man at the plate, Beefy signaled Jones to throw his best one—a wide, sweeping crossfire, that dropped sharply as it crossed the pentagon. The batter missed it, clean, but the ball was low and hard to handle. It ricocheted off the edge of Gilman's glove and bounded along the turf behind him.

"Come on!" yelled the first-base coacher, and the Sheldon man streaked for the bag. Beefy was off balance when he overtook the bobbling sphere—off balance when he threw it. He tumbled in a ludicrous heap the instant after, but the ball traveled straight and beat the runner to first by a stride.

I looked at Red Lassiter when the umpire yelled "You're out!" The injured catcher was leaning forward from his place on the bench, cheering with all his might.

The weak end of our line-up came to bat in the last of the eighth, and we thanked fortune for that three-run lead, as we watched their feeble efforts. Sheldon's young moundsman seemed to grow stronger and surer of himself with every pitch. He fanned Rube Richards, worked Denby for a pop fly that he caught himself, and finished the inning by setting Whiff Jones down on three straight strikes.

Then came the ninth. With the score 6 to 3 in the home team's favor, you might expect some exuberance among the players when they took the field. But our boys were pretty quiet—all except Beefy Gilman. He banged his mitt and pranced and talked it up for all he was worth.

Sheldon looked like anything but a beaten team as

their first man marched up, swinging a couple of bats. They could see what all of us knew—that Whiff Jones was a very tired pitcher. It showed in the lines of his drawn face and the labored motion of his arm.

He threw two balls—a strike—another ball.

"That's all right, Jonesy, ol' kid! Now you've got the range," called Gilman with forced cheerfulness. And Jones wound up again. It was over—a straight, slow ball with nothing on it but direction. The batter took a toe-hold and smashed it through short. He was safe on second before the ball had finished bouncing around the outfield.

The next man walked, and the Sheldon stand began a rhythmic, nerve-racking chant of "We want runs!"

They got them. Before the inning was a minute older, Powers hit a sharp single over first. One man crossed the plate and another moved to third. And poor old Whiff left the hill. He got a tremendous hand from the State crowd as he walked dejectedly toward the showers, but that didn't help the look of things. There we were with a third-string pitcher and a catcher who had never played before in a big game—a fast-vanishing lead— two of the enemy on bases—and none out.

Johnny Ray warmed up, obviously nervous. He had plenty of speed and under ordinary conditions his control was good. But the first ball he threw was almost a wild pitch. Beefy made a heroic jump for it and managed to pull it down, but by that time the speedy Powers was well on his way to second. A throw was out of the question.

With hostile runners dancing like Indians on second and third, Ray had trouble finding the range. Two more balls came over and then a strike. The next one scorched across the plate, knee-high, but to the intense disgust of our rooters, the umpire called it low. The bases were loaded and our first put-out was still to be made.

I gave a groan as I saw the Sheldon players cavorting around their bench. There was another heavy hitter at the plate, swinging his bat confidently. A slaughter was imminent and I hated to watch it.

At any rate, I didn't have long to wait. On the first ball pitched, a high fly went sailing deep into center-field. The Sheldon runners held their bases while Deuce Diamond raced backward, yard after dizzy yard. At last it came down in his hands but he was far away. With the tired centerfielder's throw, Powers, on second, and the man on third started their sprint. Joe Dove got the ball too late to stop either of them. The run came in, and there was the dangerous Powers perched on the hot corner. Score, 6 to 5, and only one down.

There was an infield conference while Beefy stood guard at the plate. The boys must have done their best

IN THE SAME SPLIT SECOND POWERS' SPIKES CUT
HIM DOWN

to buck the pitcher up, but when a team has the scent of victory in its nostrils, it's hard to stop.

"Come on and play ball!" yelled a new Sheldon batter, pawing the earth with his cleats, and the fielders returned to their places.

Contrary to all the rules of score-keeping, I shut my eyes when Johnny Ray delivered the next pitch. But I couldn't help bearing the sickening crack of wood on horsehide. The hit was a smoking grounder to Bert Kane, off first. He snapped it up, on the run, and touched the base in two strides.

"Quick—home it!" Beefy Gilman piped, for Powers was tearing in from third like an express train. It's no joke to stand sidewise in the path of a charging base-runner and wait for a throw. Gilman did it, blocking the lane with his burly body. The ball came to him and in the same split second Powers' spikes cut him down. But he tagged him as he fell, and when the dust cleared, there was the Sheldon runner's foot still inches away from the plate.

I'm not going to try to describe the jubilation of the next few minutes. Winning a ball-game with a climax as wild as that is bound to go to people's heads. I got as much kick out of it as anybody, thinking how old Beefy had won his letter at last.

But the biggest thrill I got that afternoon was still

to come. No one else shared it with me because no one else noticed. Just as the mob was pouring on the field, I saw Lassiter race out from the bench to pound Gilman on the back. And it came over me suddenly that the red-head wasn't limping.

I made a quick break through the crowd and caught up with Bill Ginty. "Coach!" I gasped. "Did you see what I saw? Red Lassiter was running on that ankle! Tell me—didn't he really—"

Ginty turned on me ferociously. "Shut up!" he snapped. And then one of his little blue eyes closed in a wink. "Young fellow," he said, more softly, "there are some things it's good to know, but not so good to talk about. Keep this out o' your paper."

That's why only three people ever knew what kept State's star catcher from running his string to 300 innings. But as far as my own opinion of him was concerned, Red Lassiter had set a record that would last a lifetime.

THE BUSH

THE BOY flicked a speck of dust off his handsome brown flannel jacket and yawned. His wrist watch showed him it was eight o'clock, though he never would have guessed it from the bright afternoon light outside. In fifteen minutes the train would be due at Lac Rideaux. He picked up his magazines languidly and stuffed them into one of his traveling-bags. Big, expensive bags they were—pigskin with gold-plated fittings. On their sides were neatly embossed letters—"L. G. C." Those were his initials. They stood for Lucius Gerald Castleman.

The porter grinned down at him. "You gettin' off, nex' stop?" he asked.

"Lac Rideaux," Luke nodded, and rose to be brushed off.

"Yassuh!" the darky chuckled. "You goin' to find yo'self right in the middle o' the bush!"

When the bags had been removed to the vestibule, Luke sat down again to wait. The same landscape he had watched at intervals all day was still rolling by. Grim-looking, ragged spruces growing on the edges of swamps and the sides of rough ravines. Small, lonely lakes. Winding streams full of snags and fallen trees.

"The bush," he said to himself with a superior smile. "They can have it."

He had first heard the word used in the dining-car at breakfast. Some mining-engineer talking to a tenderfoot across the coffee and eggs. "Wait till you get in there a few miles," he had said. "Then you'll know what the bush is like."

As one who had been to Switzerland and Glacier Park, and taken an auto trip through the California redwoods, Luke was unimpressed by this northern Ontario country. Really, he couldn't see why his father had wanted him to come up here. There were no majestic mountains, no giant trees, no real scenery.

At first he had found a thrill in the tiny settlements along the single track. Most of them had a Hudson's Bay Company store, a dozen low log houses, and a red frame station building, huddled at the edge of the woods. A few roughly dressed white men and Indians lounged on the platform, and there were big mongrel dogs sniffing at such passengers as got out to stretch their legs. But after eight or ten hours, these scenes had become monotonous.

The train slowed down and Luke went back to the door. Strung out along the track, the cabins of Lac

Rideaux looked very much like all the other stops. The only difference Luke noticed was a broad sheet of water glinting red in the sunset. As he stood there on the platform beside his luggage, a lanky youngster in ill-fitting store clothes and a gray cap approached. He was about Luke's age, but taller. He had sun-bleached brown hair, and his skin was burned a deep red brown.

The stranger sized Luke up with steady blue eyes. "You lookin' for Crombies'?" he asked.

"Yes," the city boy replied. "My father wrote you about my coming. I'm Luke Castleman." He spoke the name with due importance. At prep school and in the Long Island younger set it meant something.

The other lad nodded. "I'm Donald Crombie," he returned. "Dad told me to take care o' you. This your stuff?"

He picked up one of the two bags and walked off, evidently expecting Luke to take the other. The heir to the Castleman fortune looked around in vain for a red-cap. Somewhat ruffled, he seized the heavy valise and followed.

Young Crombie led the way back along the settlement's single dirt street, and stopped in front of a neat log house. "Mrs. MacRae, here, takes lodgers," he announced. "She'll put you up tonight an' we'll get off in the morning. Had supper?"

"I dined on the train," Luke answered stiffly.

"A good thing," said Donald. "The grub in the station lunchroom ain't much to brag about. I'll bring a duffle-bag up here to put your things in, 'round seven tomorrow. I suppose you've got flannel shirts—breeches —high boots—regular woods outfit? Okay. See you in the morning."

Luke knocked on the door and was admitted by the elderly Scotchwoman. In the small, clean bedroom to which she led him, he unpacked his clothes and the things he wanted to take into the bush. Later he went out for a walk.

It was ten o'clock but the northern twilight still hung over the settlement. He strolled northward a hundred yards and passed the last of the log houses. Beyond was a brief space of stump pasture where a cow-bell tinkled mournfully. Then the dark, forbidding wall of the forest. It looked wild enough in that weird half-light. Maybe it wouldn't be so bad up here, after all. Luke had been rather scornful when his father suggested the trip. What he had wanted was a month at a dude ranch in Wyoming. Ho, hum! He returned to Mrs. MacRae's and went to bed.

Don Crombie, looking somehow bigger and more at ease in his woods clothes, called for him at what seemed a very early hour. Cheerfully, the young guide helped him stow his belongings in the duffle-bag. He looked approvingly at Luke's expensive boots and fine trout-rod. "That's a dandy camera, too," he said. "Bring it along. We might catch sight of a moose."

They stopped at the station for a plate of ham and eggs, then proceeded to a long shed by the landing-dock.

"Our storehouse," said Don proudly. "We outfit twenty or thirty parties a year, here."

He swung a twenty-foot canoe out of the rack and moored it by the dock. "Now pass me those things as I call for 'em," he commanded.

Luke repressed a desire to ask him who his servant was last year, and did as he was ordered. Boxes, bags, bed-rolls and a light wall tent were packed amidships. An ax, a rifle, paddles and setting-poles completed the cargo.

"Okay," said Crombie. "Take the bow, an' we'll start."

An Indian, lounging against the shed wall, grinned and waved good-by to them. Otherwise no stir was created by their departure.

A gentle southerly breeze favored them all that morning and they had made more than twenty miles when Don steered in toward a wooded point.

"We'll get lunch here," he said. "Then we can camp

at the foot o' the lake tonight. Down Reckless River it's a hundred an' fifty miles to the Albany. We can come back up the Kamwash by way o' Loon Lake, an' it'll make just a nice three weeks' trip."

Luke had done some paddling in Maine and the Adirondacks, but five solid hours of it had put an ache in his shoulders. He was glad to lie on a ledge in the sun and let Don prepare the meal. The young guide lost no time about it. He split a jack-pine log twice with his ax, made kindling out of one of the quarters, and whittled a thick plume of shavings at one end of a stick. A single match sufficed to set the resinous splints alight. He piled the kindling tent-wise around the little blaze and in two minutes had an excellent fire.

Plenty of butter went into the skillet. Then corned beef hash out of a tin. Four fresh eggs were fried, and Don deftly cut big slices of bread with his hunting knife. "All right," he called cheerfully, "let's eat."

With the wind still aiding them, they reached the end of the lake by five that afternoon, and Don steered the craft into a narrow outlet stream.

"The first carry's only a couple o' miles down, an' there's a good camping place at the foot of it," he explained. At the moment Luke was too tired to care. They landed at the head of a rough-looking rapid, and began unloading the canoe.

"Three trips ought to do it," said Don in a matter-of-fact tone. "You take a shoulder-pack an' one bed-roll."

The city boy struggled into the straps of a heavy knapsack and swung the cumbersome bulk of a sleeping-bag over his shoulder. The guide meanwhile had burdened himself with a hundred-pound grub-box and two or three other items, slung from his head by a tump-line. He strode away over a narrow trail, with Luke staggering in pursuit.

That portage was the roughest walking he had ever encountered, and apparently it had no end. In places he waded through wet muck that came nearly to the tops of his boots. Then there would be a ledge to scramble over, or a few fallen logs, sprawled knee-high across the path.

At last he saw open water through the trees, and Crombie easing down his pack on the bank.

"Say—" Luke panted—"how far did we come?"

Don laughed. "Tired?" he asked. "Sit down an' rest while I make the next trip. This isn't much of a portage—less'n half a mile. We'll have some that are two miles long."

Luke didn't sit down. He followed the other boy doggedly along the back trail, and again loaded himself with duffle.

"This isn't bad," Don encouraged him. "You ought to try it in June, when the mosquitoes get in your eyes an' down your throat!"

Luke gritted his teeth and tried to keep pace with his guide's long, easy strides. He was all in when they reached the end of the carry, but he had not stopped to rest or fallen behind.

"Say—you do all right for a tenderfoot," Don grinned at him. "That's all there is to pack except the canoe. I can handle that myself."

Luke lay back against a stump and forgot his weary muscles in watching a pair of wood-ducks that swam in the still pool below the bank. After a quarter of an hour he heard a heavy tread and looked up to see Don approaching like a great green beetle under the shell of the canoe.

"Feel better?" the young woodsman asked. "Here— fix up your rod an' catch us a trout for supper while I make camp. Just above, there, at the foot o' the rapids, you ought to find a fish."

Luke chose a brown hackle out of his fly-book and made a few casts. At the fourth try, there was a flash of silver spray and a speckled monster took the lure. A hundred feet of line sang out and then Luke was reeling frantically. He played the fish for twenty minutes and his arms felt ready to drop off. Twice he was on the point of yelling to Don for aid, but his stubborn pride restrained him. If he was tired, the trout was tired, too. The rushes were shorter now, and the rests longer. He reeled in against the fish and saw the big, gleaming body struggling feebly, almost at his feet. Don was there with the landing-net.

"Nice fish," the woods boy commented, holding it up. "Round about four pounds."

Luke's eyes bulged. "Why, that must be a record!" he panted. "I never heard of a speckled trout that big!"

"A good one, all right," Don smiled, "but not real big for this country. One o' my sports got an eleven-pounder last year."

Luke relapsed into resentful silence. He was too nearly all in to argue but he felt injured over the casual way Crombie had treated his trout. Leaning back against a log, he watched the preparations for supper.

Don had cleaned the fish with half a dozen quick motions. Now he laid the thick, pink trout-steaks in the pan, and a subtle fragrance filled the air. The coffee-pot bubbled cheerfully in the embers. Luke began to feel more friendly toward the world.

By the time he had finished an excellent supper, some of the ache of weariness had gone out of his back and shoulders. He even offered to help wash the dishes, but Don told him to sit still.

"This ain't much of a job," said the guide. "Take off your boots an' I'll get 'em greased up for tomorrow. We'll hit some muskeg on the next portage."

In the dusk a brown snowshoe rabbit came hopping out of the undergrowth to sniff at the campers inquisitively. Its immense, furry hind feet made a rustling sound on the twigs. Don sat quiet, holding out a bit of bread and at last the visitor came close enough to nibble at the food. Then Luke moved a little and the rabbit was gone in a flash.

It grew cold after sunset. The warmth of an eiderdown sleeping-bag was pleasant, and the springy balsam boughs Don had gathered made a comfortable bed. In two minutes both boys were asleep.

The long night's rest did Luke a lot of good. He woke at the sound of Don's ax, and came out blinking in the early sun. The still brown water of the pool looked tempting.

"Guess I'll take a swim," he remarked, rubbing his bare body.

"I'm afraid you'll find it a mite cold," the woods boy answered. "Don't know as I would, if I were you."

Luke's stubborn streak was roused at once. He ran down the ledge and took off in a long, shallow dive. His hands, stretched in front of him, encountered some kind of slimy water-weed, and his knee scraped on a sunken log. He knew at once that only luck had kept him from breaking his neck. But the shock of the icy water drove even that thought from his head. He turned, thrashing back to shore with frantic strokes. When he hauled himself out on the ledge again, he was shivering so hard his teeth rattled.

"Keep runnin' around!" said Crombie. "Start your circulation goin'. I'll get you a towel."

Luke danced up and down the ledge, rubbed himself violently with the turkish towel, and finally felt a glow of warmth in his reddened limbs.

"Feelin' better?" grinned the guide, dexterously tossing a flap-jack.

"Yes." Luke's reply was gruff. He hated to make a fool of himself.

All that day they went on down the river. Moose sign was everywhere along the portages. Several times when they were toiling through swampy muskeg, Don stopped and pointed to tracks—great, deep prints of splay hooves in the mud. "You better keep that camera ready," he advised. "Might see one any time now."

Grudgingly, the city boy admitted to himself that this voyaging through the wilderness was fun. "How far have we come from Lac Rideaux?" he asked that night by the camp-fire.

"Sixty-five or seventy miles," Don answered.

"And we haven't seen a human being—or a road—or a house," Luke marveled.

"Not likely to, in this far," said the guide. "Nearest settlement beyond here is Fort Churchill, up on Hudson Bay. We might come across an Indian or two, but that's all."

Luke's eagerness to get a picture of a moose increased as the third morning wore on. Twice they heard the crash of big bodies in the brush on shore, and several times bits of grass floating in the water had shown them where moose had been feeding a few minutes before. At each bend of the river the boy stared ahead expectantly. His camera lay in the peak of the bow between his feet, ready for instant use.

"We're comin' to a rapids now," Crombie called from the stern. "Not bad, except there's a big rock at the foot. Get ready to paddle hard on the left when I tell you."

Luke eyed the stretch of white water without alarm. He had shot stiffer rapids in Maine. The canoe slipped down fast between the high spruce-clad banks. Looking ahead, the city boy could see a still pool below and—he stared—yes, a huge black bull browsing knee-deep in the water-grass!

Hastily he reached forward and seized the camera. For a moment he could not locate the moose in the finder. Then he had it. The big head with its spread of fuzzy antlers was lifted in alarm. Luke clicked the shutter and turned the film swiftly. They were closer now, and he could get a beautiful shot as the moose left the water.

"Paddle!" yelled Don behind him. Luke waited a second till the big beast was squarely in the finder, then snapped the shutter again. When he put down the camera and grabbed for his paddle, he realized something was wrong. The frail craft under him was slipping sidewise like a skidding car. An eddy had caught them and was sweeping the stern in toward the big rock.

Before Luke could dip the ash blade they struck with a splintering crash. The canoe lurched to the shock, nearly tipped over, then righted itself again, hanging fast on a jagged knee of rock. Guiltily the boy looked back.

Don Crombie had been thrown half over the gunwale and still sprawled there, a broken paddle shaft gripped in his right hand. His left arm was crumpled queerly under him and his face was pale under the tan. With a grim effort he pulled himself back into a kneeling position. The arm still hung unnaturally at his side.

"We're all right," he spoke through clenched teeth. "There's a hole stove in the bottom, but we'll make it to shore if we can get off. Guess you'll have to do the liftin', though."

Luke's jaw dropped. "G-gosh!" he stammered. "Your arm's broken! I—I'm sorry, Don."

He took his paddle and climbed gingerly back across the tarpaulin-covered duffle.

"You can stand on the rock," Don said. "I'll go up to the bow. Then you shove off an' get ready to steer."

Luke got a foothold on the slippery boulder and held fast to the gunwale while the injured guide crawled painfully forward.

"All right," Don told him laconically. He heaved with all his strength and freed the canoe—then stepped in, as the stern shot by. They gathered swift headway in the final chute of the rapids, and their momentum carried them quickly across the pool. Luke beached the craft and stepped out in the shallow water.

Ten minutes later he had helped Crombie up the bank to a resting place under the trees, and had laid out the duffle to dry. A huge gap in the side of the canoe had let in several inches of water before they reached shore.

Sober-faced, the city boy stood before his guide. "That was my fault," he gulped. "And I'll never forgive myself."

"Forget it," Don answered with a twisted grin. "Let's

THE FRAIL CRAFT WAS SLIPPING SIDEWISE

figure what's to be done. Maybe things aren't as bad as they look."

But as they discussed the situation, Luke began to realize its full significance. They were more than a hundred miles from the nearest settlement. Their canoe was damaged beyond ordinary patching. And Don was not only disabled but in grave need of a surgeon. Both bones of his fore-arm had been snapped between the gunwale and the rock as he tried to fend them off with the paddle. He made no complaint, but Luke knew from the tense white line of his jaw that he was in agony.

"I reckon," the woods boy said, at length, "this thing has got to be set somehow. Think you could do it?"

"I'll try," Luke answered. But his fingers trembled as he touched the fracture, and when the other boy winced he stood back, shaking his head.

"All right," Don panted. "There's one other way— if you only knew the woods. Dad's got a party coming up the Kamwash. There's a Dr. Raeburn with 'em—a famous doctor from Chicago. If they're on schedule they'll be camped at Porcupine Rapids tonight. That's twenty miles straight north through the bush. But it's tough going—afoot—"

"I'll go!" Luke exclaimed. "I'll get there—if you can make out here alone."

It was nearly noon then. Nine hours of daylight left. He set to work furiously, putting up the tent—chopping firewood—making a sling for Don's arm out of a spare shirt—packing a knapsack for himself.

A furious energy made up for his awkwardness. He cut a pile of boughs for the bed-place and saw that his companion was as comfortable as he could be made. Then he slung the pack on his shoulders.

"Wish I had a compass to give you," Don said. "Keep the sun behind you the first couple of hours. Then over your left shoulder. When it sets, it'll be square on your left. There's no big stream till you come to the Kamwash, but you may strike some brooks and a pond or two. With good luck you ought to make the river by sundown. Then keep headin' upstream. There's a portage trail the length of the rapids an' they'll be camped at one end or the other. If they're not there, wait for 'em. Dad'll know the quickest way to get back here."

He sank back on the boughs, gritting his teeth with pain. And Luke said good-by.

He didn't cast about for an easy way into the bush, but plunged straight into the tangled undergrowth. He had two days' rations and a match-safe in his pack—a small hand-ax stuck in his belt. With that equipment he was pitting his inexperience against the wilderness. If he had known more about this undertaking, perhaps he might have been afraid. As it was, he had no time to think of anything but the immediate business of smashing his way through the brush.

The first mile or two was made difficult by dense coverts of young spruce—"rabbit-bush" as Don had called them. Only a rabbit or a weasel could have gone through such places, and Luke was forced continually to find a way around. Often the taller trees hid the sun so completely that he worried about losing his bearings.

At last he came to higher, more open ground, where rocky ledges and fallen trees were his only obstacles. He made better time there. When his wrist watch told him it was three o'clock he figured he had come five miles. A quarter of the distance, and he was already tired!

After another hour he sat down on a rotting log to rest and get his breath. It was very still in the woods. The soft *hush—hush* of wind far above in the spruce tops, and an occasional drowsy cheeping of birds seemed to make the silence more intense. Even the Canada jay that had followed him, scolding, the first few miles from camp, had now deserted him.

His throat was dry. He hoped he'd strike some water soon. Ten minutes later his wish was ironically fulfilled. He came down a steep slope and looked eagerly for a brook at the bottom. Instead, his boots began to squelch in soft muck. He was at the edge of a muskeg swamp.

Dreary-looking tamaracks were all around him now —tall ghosts of trees, draped with gray "squaw's whiskers." Thirsty as he was, he had no desire to drink from the stagnant pools that gleamed on every side. He plowed doggedly ahead, stepping on tussocks of swamp-grass, sunken logs—anything that offered a footing. It was impossible to hold a straight course, but he tried to keep his shadow diagonally forward and to the right. How far did this muskeg reach, he wondered with dread. It was like a nightmare—the yielding, soaking moss that clutched at his feet—the half-dead trees—the empty sky. Suppose he should step off into one of those black, treacherous pools and begin to sink. Fear made him hesitate, his tired legs trembling. Then he thought of Don, back there by the river, and stumbled on again.

Abruptly, half a mile beyond, the muskeg gave place to dry land. He panted up a ridge, hacked his way through a spruce thicket, and descended again toward shimmering blue water. Before him was a pretty little lake, shut in by high black forest. Gratefully, Luke ran down the bank and plunged his face into the cold water.

As he finished drinking he heard a loud snort and a mighty splash. Thirty yards up the shore a cow moose went scrambling awkwardly into the woods. The boy grinned and felt better. A look at his watch told him it was nearly six. Had he come halfway? In another three hours it would be close to sunset. He pulled a chunk of bread out of the knapsack and gnawed at it as he hurried on. There was no time to stop for a real meal.

After he had circled the pond, Luke found himself in a new kind of country. The boles of big, straight spruces shot up nearly a hundred feet without a limb, so closely were they packed together. Overhead, the tops made a solid green roof through which only a faint twilight penetrated. The ground beneath was clear of brush, and made good traveling if only he could be sure of his direction. Once, when an opening in the woods gave him a view of the sinking sun, he found it was almost behind him. How long had he been bearing to the right? Panicky, he swung at a sharp angle and plodded on.

Light began to show through the trees ahead, and he emerged into a desolate tract of burned land. The fire must have swept it no more than a year before, for there were few vines or young saplings growing there. However, the going was slow. He had to clamber over charred trunks that had fallen in jumbled heaps. A mile of it and his hands and breeches were black.

Small streams began to cut across his path. Some of them were too broad to jump, and he waded above his boot-tops to reach the farther bank. He was desperately tired now. With increasing frequency his heavy feet tripped over roots and branches. After one of these tumbles he lay still, wondering if he would ever find strength to get up again. Then, hardly knowing how he did it, he was on his feet and lurching forward.

Those last two hours were always hazy in Luke's mind. He could remember coming to a narrow lake that he took at first for the Kamwash. And he had some dim recollection of a cramp in his thigh that had stretched him on the ground in agony for precious minutes.

The sun was gone, leaving a golden glow in the west, when at last he emerged on the bank of a swift-flowing river. He turned to the left, and slowly, painfully, followed the shore upstream. There was a faint rumble in his ears that grew louder as he advanced. A yellowish mound of floating froth swept by in the river. Then, ahead, he saw the rapids—tumbling white water that roared over jagged rocks. Porcupine they called it. A swell name for those sharp, black needles. . . . He had fallen over a stump in the trail. Yes, it was a trail. Just a minute and he'd get up, but it was such a good place to rest. . . .

The next thing Luke knew, a wrinkled, copper-hued face bent above him and a hand was shaking his shoulder. "Hey!" called a voice. "Dis fella, she's 'sleep on de portage!"

Other figures surrounded him, as the boy struggled to his knees.

"Is—is Mr. Crombie here?" he asked.

A big man beside him nodded. "Right here."

And Luke gasped out his story. "Don's camped on Reckless River, at the foot of a rapids," he concluded. "His arm is pretty bad, I'm afraid. The end of the bone was almost coming through the skin. He said you'd know how to get the doctor there the quickest way."

"Yes," said Don's father. "You'll stay with the party, here, and we'll meet you at Lac Rideaux. Dr. Raeburn, if you don't mind traveling tonight we can get there by morning. Just above here there's a stream big enough for a canoe, and barring one or two carries we can go all the way by water. You Tom, and Louis," he spoke to the guides, "take good care of this boy. He's done quite a job today."

.   .   .   .

A night's sleep made Luke practically as good as new. There was a stiffness in his leg muscles and an ache in his back, but he had an appetite that made even the Indian guides marvel. The party went on, that forenoon, poling up-river by easy stages. And three days later they were paddling across from the Kamwash to Lac Rideaux through a chain of small lakes and rivers.

Luke packed his share of the duffle over the last carry,

and the three canoes shot down a winding stream into the big lake. One of the guides pointed off to the northeast. There was a dark speck in the blue expanse, and a rhythmic flash of lifted paddles. Gradually the canoes drew closer and Luke could see three figures in the approaching craft. The one in the middle waved, and a cheerful hail came across the water.

"It's Don!" he cried. "They got him, all right. Hi, boy!"

The flotilla pulled alongside and Don Crombie stretched out his right hand to seize Luke's. The other arm was heavy with splints and bandages.

"We made it by morning," Don's father was saying. "None too soon, either. The lad was out of his head with fever, and the arm had swelled up bad. But he's in fine shape now, thanks to the doctor and this young bush-cruiser, here."

Don grinned. "A good thing for me I had a real woodsman along," he said.

Luke shook his head. There was a lump in his throat, but he was prouder of that compliment than of any ever paid him.

"I guess," he said humbly, "the bush must do something to a guy like me. What do you say, Don—will you take me in again next year?"

STRAWS IN THE WIND

KAY EMERGED, inch by greasy inch, from the black depths beneath the engine, and squirmed to a sitting position beside the left headlight. Around him on the garage floor lay the implements of his assault. Triumphantly he rubbed his nose with a smudgy forefinger, and thumped a worn tire with the heel of his hand.

"There," he addressed the car, "I've fixed *you*, by the Great Hook Block!"

The expletive had, of course, no relation to the mechanical feat just accomplished. It was a phrase picked up years before from "Captains Courageous," and he took an epicure's satisfaction in its fine salty flavor as he rolled it on his tongue. Kay would be seventeen next month. He was wiry and tow-headed and had an inquiring blue eye.

As he stood wiping his tools by the dusty window, he could catch dim glimpses of the New Hampshire hills, purple with distance. Nearer by was the undulating green stubble of the mowing-field, with the corn-patch beyond. And there, of a sudden, sitting high on a knoll at the edge of the waving corn, was the woodchuck.

Kay crossed the yard in stealthy haste and dashed upstairs to his room. From the collection of new, second-hand and antique firearms laid in racks along the wall, he selected the one gun that would really shoot—his trusty twenty-two.

Down past the hollyhocks and the chicken-house he sped, taking advantage of every natural cover to hide him from his arch-enemy, then clambered silently and with bated breath over the pasture wall. Along its lower side he stole, bent low, his moccasined feet melting into the grass like an Indian's.

At last he was opposite the cornfield. He climbed the wall once more, with infinite care lest he disturb a stone, and moved feather-footed into the high corn. There was a little breeze that rustled the leaves constantly and drowned the noise of his advance. Within four rows of the edge he stopped, for he could begin to see the grass beyond. His heart was beating so fiercely that he could feel the quick, regular catch in his breathing. He knelt down, so as to peer between the lower stalks. And there, barely thirty feet away, with fat and contemptuous gray back turned toward the corn-patch, sat the woodchuck.

It was perhaps the twentieth time that Kay had stalked him that summer, but never before had there been a

MOVED FEATHER-FOOTED INTO THE HIGH CORN

shot like this. A moment the boy waited, to down the buck-fever that was mounting in his veins. Then he raised the rifle slowly and brought a perfect bead to bear on the middle of the furry back. Or should he try for that wee glimpse of the head that showed beyond? He shifted the muzzle a hair's breadth, and—

"Kay!" came a feminine call from the direction of the house. The woodchuck turned with incredible haste and no dignity whatever, and dove incontinent into his burrow, just as Kay pulled the trigger.

"Kay," called his older sister's voice again. "Time to milk!" and then, "Did you get him?"

Of what use were words? The young hunter turned silently on his heel, cast backward toward the house one look of ineffable disgust, and climbed over the pasture wall.

Clear to the foot of the hill this feeling remained with him, and his scorn for all the weaker sex was reflected in the remarks he addressed to Brownie and Lily Bell, ruminating in the brook-bed.

"Ah, Ladies," said he with biting sarcasm, "as far as possible from the barn, I see." And he threw a small green apple with vicious accuracy at the placid rump of Lily Bell.

"Hurr'up!" he cried fiercely. "Hurr'up along!" The cows obeyed with alacrity, and appeased by the sight of their lumbering haste he turned from wrath and began to whistle.

Kay did not enjoy milking. He had, in fact, hated it with a whole-souled hatred until he discovered that it hardened his forearms. After that he performed it as an unpleasant sort of calisthenic exercise, and took comfort in feeling of the corded muscles when no one was watching.

Another palliative there was, also. One had to wear a special set of old clothes while milking, and Kay had devised a costume that was gloriously buccaneerish. He tucked his overalls into a huge pair of old-fashioned sea boots, donned a brass-buttoned jumper and a red neckerchief, and pulled a villainous old slouch hat over his right eye. In this garb he felt more at liberty to sing "Fifteen Men" and "Barnacle Bill" while he milked. The cows seemed to have no objection to these incongruous themes, but gave down their milk as merrily as if they had been born to the bounding main.

The girls had set the table and supper-getting was well under way when he poured out his warm, white panfuls in the kitchen. To the frivolous remarks that were addressed to him he opposed a dignified silence, and departed upstairs to change his clothes. This required time. His mother, who saw him only during vacations, never quite believed the story he told of rising with the warning bell at school, and being washed, dressed and inside the dining-hall when the final call came, five minutes later.

Kay would have punched the head of anyone who accused him of being vain. His contempt for sissies who spent time in slicking back their hair knew no bounds. But when, stripped to the waist, he caught a glimpse of his shining torso in the mirror, he must needs stand before it for a moment or two. His stomach muscles played beautifully, in solid rectangular lumps beneath the skin. The biceps and shoulder muscles bunched themselves obligingly, as he flexed or extended his arms. His chest filled out, deep and square, as he drew great breaths. Yet Kay was not engrossed in these details. He frowned. Fourteen— Gee, what a size to have your collar-band! He thought of Bull Olafsson, who played fullback on the school team. There was a neck! Sixteen and a half! He must work out some sort of head-bending exercises that would swell his neck muscles. Let's see—left—back—right—back—front—back—how would that work? He would do it every morning when he got up. Too bad he hadn't begun earlier. And anyhow, Dave mustn't see the collar-size on those shirts.

For the first time, perhaps, in his life, Kay carefully removed the miscellany of soiled linen from hooks and chairs, and stuffed it into a drawer of the bureau. When one has an older brother who broke the intercollegiate pole-vault record, and that brother is about to come home for his first visit in a year, physical scandals like a size-fourteen neck must be kept concealed, even at the cost of tradition and precedent.

Kay reached the supper table late, which was not unusual. His sisters smiled sweetly.

"Well," said Lois, "here's our young hunter! What's been keeping him all this time?"

"Probably busy counting the heads of game," suggested Anne, and coughed behind her hand.

The youth meanwhile accepted his filled plate with great unconcern, and let no jibes disturb his demolition of baked beans and buttered brown bread.

Supper was done and the dishes cleared away when Kay slipped out through the cool, gathering dusk to talk to the colts. In his hand he carried two early apples. He came up to the wall where the black head and the bay hung over, and soft whickerings arose. When the apples had been broken, he held a piece first to one pair of eager, fumbling, velvet lips, then to the other, till his gifts had been shared equally. He murmured caressing nothings that held them fascinated for a little. Finally the black colt gave his slender head a toss, and off they both went at a trot, down the ravine. And evening descended, behind the great spreading tops of the elms.

On Kay fell the vague yearning that comes at the end or at the beginning of things. He went into the house.

.   .   .   .

An hour later, buried in the advertising pages of a magazine, Kay's ear was caught by something his mother was saying.

"But it's honorable!" she exclaimed. "Teaching is the kind of work that any gentleman can be proud of, if he puts his ideals into it. And besides, Anne, why do you say his success in tinkering with the car proves that he was born to build engines? Isn't it just as much the sort of instinct that a doctor must have? There's been at least one professional man in the family for six generations, and now that Dave's gone into the advertising business"—she spoke with a faint distaste—"it makes me all the more anxious for Kay to follow the law, or medicine, or teaching. *I* think he would make a lovely minister."

With the latter pronouncement she lowered her voice and stole a look in her son's direction. All was well. He appeared even more than commonly immersed in his magazine.

"Yes—but, Mother," said Lois, impatiently, "all that is so vague, and so old-fashioned, don't you see? There—

now I've hurt your feelings, but you know 'professions' *are* old-fashioned. And he must decide now—*must* begin training himself for his life's work. Don't you understand? Modern competition has broken into your genteel old professions, even."

She glanced down at the treatise on Vocations she had been reading, and thumbed the pages swiftly. "Here," she went on, "it's just as this book says—'The great successes of the future will be men and women whose every action is watched from childhood, and who are trained rigorously along the line of their greatest aptitude.' And just think—he'll be seventeen in four weeks and we've hardly *begun!* Anne and I only realized our responsibility a little over a month ago, and there were so many Minor Tendencies that we couldn't make sure of his Dominant Trait for ever so long."

Anne broke in eagerly. "Lois is right, Mother. I found a new vocational book called 'Square Pegs' at the Library. It says that every boy who expects to be a success should know exactly what career lies ahead of him, and be definitely shaping himself for it, before he's eighteen. By then he should have his whole soul on fire with the work he is to do. Oh, I know what it must be to dream great bridges and power-plants and railroad systems, and then to watch them come true in steel and concrete! How can you put a Technocrat below a lawyer, Mother? And besides, Kay has never shown any interest in law, or the ministry, or medicine, for that matter, and he just *loves* machinery—don't you, Kay?" she threw over her shoulder.

The answer was a sort of subdued grunt, indicating the extreme of inattention, and Lois returned to the assault.

"You see we must watch for these tendencies, Mother. They are what this book of mine calls 'Straws in the Wind.' They show which way his latent abilities point. Every preference a boy shows for one kind of vocation is valuable. And as soon as possible it should be given intelligent direction. That's the modern system. I wish Kay were ready to enter Tech this fall, though of course he has to finish prep school first. But at Tech they'll put him right where he belongs, and train him to the height of efficiency in his line. Engineering *is* the line, all right, Mother. Anne thinks it's Mechanical Engineering, but more of my own data points toward the Electrical branch. Don't you remember how he fixed the door-bell, when the wire was disconnected or something?"

It was at this juncture that Father woke from his doze in the arm-chair with a series of snorts.

"What's this you girls are talking about?" he rumbled. "Why, that's all nonsense. Kay's going to be a farmer. Right down in this state we've got as good an agricultural school as you'll find anywhere. It won't cost him much to go there, and there's going to be good money in farming a few years from now—soon as taxes and prices get straightened out. The man who goes at it scientifically and is willing to work can clean up a tidy pile—and he'll always eat! Wish I'd sold the furniture business sooner and gone at it myself. Right here's eighty acres of the best land in the state, to start with, and it can be made the nucleus of a big place—a *big* place, and big business.

"What's going to happen if all the boys go to the cities to earn their living?" he asked belligerently. "Some of the old stock has got to stay right here in the state, on the farms, and be the backbone of the nation."

"Oh, but Father, listen," began both girls at once. "You don't see it right—" "You haven't the modern viewpoint—" "Kay hasn't shown a *bent* for farming! Tell him yourself, Kay—"

But Kay was not there.

He was running through the tall, wet hollyhocks by the chicken-yard. Out he went, without slackening pace, till he reached the farthest field, and stood alone in the moon-bathed night. The still, white beauty struck him poignantly. Something seemed to be choking him, and he had to wink hard to keep back unmanly tears.

What was the use of being nearly seventeen if all

his remaining days were to be spent plodding a road that someone else had laid out for him in advance? It was no good telling himself that his family meant well. Of course they did. A sense of their real affection brought a lump in his throat. The finest family a man ever had! But all this talk of theirs was making him hate the very word "career." After all, it was *his* life they were messing with. Why couldn't they leave a guy something?

Kay clenched his fists and drew a deep breath. "Just a little more—" he muttered fiercely, "just a couple of peeps more out of those girls—and I'll show 'em!"

The wide sweep of the hills under the moon beckoned him, thrilling and mysterious. Somewhere out there in the silent, shimmering vastness was the answer to his trouble. All the secrets of that undiscovered country would be his one day, and in it he would fight for a place of his own making.

But first there were specific things that he wanted from life and meant to have, in spite of all the vocational books in the libraries. One was college. Not the high-voltage "training for a career" that Anne and Lois talked about, but four years such as Dave had known. The glorious struggle for a place on the teams, the fierce loyalties to college and class, the friendships and the "bull-sessions," the contact with wise and understanding professors, the long browsings among books. Four years in which to find himself!

Kay set his jaw and went down the hill till he stood by the pasture fence, where the river gleamed through the pines. Beside the shining water ran the straight, bright threads of the railroad. They led on and on, to the horizon and over it, to Boston and New York and all the world.

Hours later, when the moon was setting, the night freight would go by, down the valley. He had lain awake many times and heard the long wail of it, whistling for the lower crossing. One who ran swiftly and leaped just at the right time and clutched with strong fingers at a flying iron hand-bar could mount the train and ride it far before morning. Beyond, there would be other railroads with other freights jolting their way west. Friendly truck-drivers would give a hitch-hiker a lift. And somewhere, a long distance off, would be a place where a man—or even a boy—could find a job and live his own life.

Kay's imagination roved through Oregon orchards and California orange groves. He saw himself riding the range on a buckskin cayuse—standing watch aboard a Pacific cargo-boat. In two or three years he could probably save as much money as he needed. And the spring that he was twenty he would come back.

Kay rather relished the thought of that return. A well-set-up young man, dressed with quiet good taste, would knock at the door one day and disclose his identity to an astounded family. Later he would respectfully but firmly inform them that he was a registered first-year man at the old college. Opening his coat he would display large class numerals earned on the gridiron, and possibly a medal won by his work in the classroom. He was about to elaborate this picture still further when he heard a contemptuous chuckle behind him. He jumped, guiltily, and looked about. In the uncertain moonlight a black figure with a white shirt-front seemed to loom beyond the fence. Again came the chuckle, but this time it was a snort, and the Perkins' black cow shook her broad, white face and went back to her night feeding.

"Hello-o-o-o, Kay!" sounded an old, familiar call from up by the house. Kay grinned happily. It was his brother's voice. He sent back an answering shout, shook the night chill out of his legs, and started at a lope up the hill. Dave met him at the fence and flung an arm about his shoulders. Approvingly he measured their breadth.

"Getting ready to be a halfback next year, are you?" he laughed. "Good old boy!"

They walked back slowly and for a while in silence.

There was real understanding between these two. When Dave spoke again it was as if he had been listening to Kay's thoughts.

"Gee, boy," he mused. "I'd like to be in your boots. You've got a great four years ahead of you!"

Kay was quiet. "The things you'll get in college won't be measurable in money," Dave continued. "They'll be bigger than money. I'm earning enough myself, now, to say that without its sounding like sour grapes. You'll just live, with all that's in you, every minute of the time. In some ways I think the best of it all comes at the end, when you make your choice of a job, and say good-by to the old crowd, and square away on your own. You'll have the pride and intelligence and courage and staying power, then, that will keep you going till you reach the top.

"You see college is going to give you—among other things—a chance to try yourself out. Do you know, at this minute, Kay, what you want to be?"

"No," answered Kay, truthfully.

"Neither did I, at your age," Dave went on. "But by Junior year I'd gone in for a lot besides track and football. I had a whack at chemistry and another at engineering. I tried running an athletic goods business, and got to be assistant baseball manager. I hustled ads for the daily, and read a little law. I took enough biology to know I wouldn't ever be a surgeon. I worked on the farm in the summer and loved it, but I was sure it wasn't my line.

"Then, by and by, I started writing stuff for the *Lit*. It went over in good shape. In Senior year, when I was put on as editor, I knew I'd found my job. It was writing. And all the other things I'd picked up gave me the kind of balance I needed to make my writing worthwhile—to myself and other people."

He paused, looking across the valley, where the moonlight touched the pines and turned them to silver and black velvet.

"You know, Kay," he said after a little, "when I asked you, a bit ago, if you knew what you wanted to be—I was ready for either sort of answer. Some fellows find out before they're out of knickerbockers. You've always had a knack for tinkering with things, but then, almost every boy has. I reckon it's just the creative instinct working itself out. Still, if you had said, back there: 'Yes, I know what I want to be. I'd give up everything for a chance to be a mechanical engineer'— well, I'd have been right with you, though I can't say I'm disappointed as it is."

"Golly!" said Kay. "It's swell that you feel that way about it. You see—" he hesitated—"Lois and Anne have kind of got in my hair. They're trying to dope out

a 'vocation' for me from some stuff they've been reading. They watch me all day long, looking for actions
the book says they ought to find. When they think they
see 'em, they call 'em 'straws in the wind' and such
hooey. I'm supposed to be a peg, and if they decide I
ought to fit a round hole then I've got to get busy and
be a round peg."

Dave gave a growl. "Listen," he said. "The country is
full of nice round pegs—as round as the technical schools
can stamp 'em. And they're out of jobs. Why? Because
most of the holes aren't round—or square—or any exact
shape that can use a machine-made peg. The good jobs
are waiting for men who have learned how to adapt
themselves—who have developed imagination and judg-
ment—human chaps with courage and horse-sense, not
cut to a pattern.

"You didn't know Billy Wentz, did you? I guess he
used to play around with me when you were a pretty
small kid. We were in prep school together. Bill's parents
decided architecture was what he was cut out for, so
when I went off to college he was entering a polytechnic
institute.

"I didn't see him again for seven or eight years. Then
one day last spring I met him, right in the middle of
Madison Square. A little seedy—a little round-shouldered

—with the look in his eyes of a man who's licked. I took him to lunch and finally got him to talk.

"He'd put in five stiff years in technical training, and had come out, I judged, a pretty good draftsman. He'd had ideas, too—it was pathetic to hear him tell about them. But he'd gone right into a job with a big concern and hadn't advanced a step, since. Same old drawing-table. Same old petty detail. Even his beginner's salary was cut, two years ago. I think he might have been a successful architect except for two things. He lacked the knowledge of how to make an impression. And he lacked confidence in himself. You can only get those qualities by experience—by knocking the corners off, to put it in peg language.

"Bill told me, so seriously it almost made me weep, that he often wondered if he wouldn't have made a better sailor than an architect. He always liked to read books about ships and the sea, he said. But after he'd put so much of his life into his training, he couldn't bring himself to turn away from it and learn something else.

"Poor old Bill! It must be a miserable feeling—never to be sure you couldn't have done better at some other job!"

They had reached the edge of the cornfield. With a chuckle, Kay brought his brother to a halt, and pointed to a hole in an earthy hillock.

"You know," he said, "the funny part of this 'straws in the wind' business is that I'd drop anything—even a monkey-wrench—to get a shot at that darned old woodchuck! According to that, it looks as if I ought to take a course in zoology, doesn't it? Or marksmanship!"

Dave whooped. "You're safe, Kay, old kid!" he laughed. "They haven't wrecked your sense of humor, anyhow."

They crossed the wet-gleaming lawn, and tramped up the steps of the porch.

"Wipe your feet, boys," called Mother. "I'm sure that grass was damp! Hadn't you both better change your shoes and stockings?"

They kissed her for answer, one on each cheek, and settled, laughing, into chairs in the circle of the reading-lamp.

Lois beamed on them with sisterly affection, and wound up a conversation which had evidently been long in progress.

"Well," she said, "we don't need to discuss it any more tonight. But some time while Dave is here we really *must* decide what Kay is to be!"

And Kay grinned happily. For his brother's left eyelid gave an almost imperceptible flicker as he nodded in solemn assent.

THE END